THE DRAGON'S DOOKIE

Other books in the FART QUEST series

Fart Quest

Fart Quest: The Barf of the Bedazzler

THE DRAGON'S DOOKIE

AARON REYNOLDS
Illustrated by Cam Kendell

Roaring Brook Press
New York

Published by Roaring Brook Press
Roaring Brook Press is a division of Holtzbrinck Publishing Holdings
Limited Partnership
120 Broadway, New York, NY 10271
mackids.com

Library of Congress Control Number: 2021906542
ISBN 978-1-250-20644-2

Our books may be purchased in bulk for promotional, educational, or business use. Please contact your local bookseller or the Macmillan Corporate
and Premium Sales Department at (800) 221-7945 ext. 5442 or by email at
MacmillanSpecialMarkets@macmillan.com.

First edition, 2022
Series design by Cassie Gonzales
Printed in the United States of America by LSC Communications,
Harrisonburg, Virginia

1   3   5   7   9   10   8   6   4   2

DWARVENFORGE ❶

KARBUNKLE
EXPANSE ❷

THE BRAMBLESHIRE ❸

CENTRAL FEY ❹

ISLE OF MOLAG ❺

ELVEN KINGDOM
OF KIRAJOY ❻

BLACKROOK
REACH ❼

CHAPTER ONE

My head is stuck in a toilet.

Why is my head in a toilet? Two words: water weirdo.

What's a water weirdo? Five words: You don't want to know.

I had never heard of a water weirdo before today. But apparently the outhouse at the Woozy Wyvern Inn has one. It keeps biting the butts of everyone who uses the facilities. And we've been hired to remove it.

"Are you sure it's still in there?" I ask, pulling my head out of the toilet.

Griff grabs tufts of his hair and tugs in frustration. Griff. Innkeeper of the Woozy Wyvern Inn. And currently, our client.

"Yes, it's in there!" he roars. "Come on, you three! I got customers! I got a reputation to uphold! I gotta do a number two!"

Let's get clear. I'm no stranger to unclogging toilets. When I was an apprentice, I had to do it once a week. Let's just say my master, Elmore the Impressive, had some impressive bowel movements.

But honestly? I thought those days were behind me. I mean, I'm a Level 3 mage, right? I'm an up-and-coming adventurer, right? I'm quickly becoming a heroic figure of myth and legend.

Right?

Nope. I'm a walking, talking potty plunger.

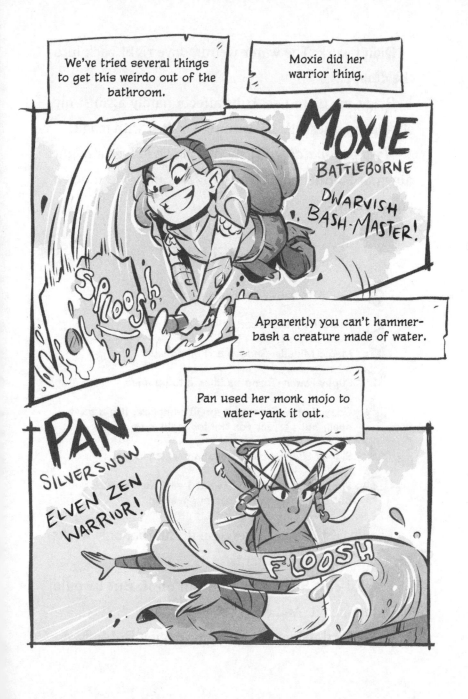

Didn't work. The water weirdo dove right back into the dumper.

Bizzy, my giant bee, rubs affectionately against my shoulder. I guess it's my turn to dazzle it with magic.

"*Pew-pew-patchoo!*" I shoot a Magic Missile straight down at it. But nada. It just fizzles into the mucky, yucky depths.

Hmm.

FART'S SPELL LIST

 Gas Attack—My trademark spell

 Feather Friend—I can talk to birds

 Magic Missile—Shoots a flaming dart

 Puppy Power—Turns baddies into puppies

 Cozy Camp—Creates a small campfire. It's a baby spell, but perfect for the job right now.

 Slip 'N Slide—Violent banana peel explosion

 Simple Suggestion—Do what I say when I touch you! But only three words per suggestion.

I could cast Feather Friend on it. But that only works on birds. Not urine serpents.

I could cast Simple Suggestion on it. But I would have to touch it. And ew.

If only I had an Incantation of Unclogging. But sadly, no.

So here we are. Still stuck with a weirdo in the outhouse.

"Come on, people!" cries Griff. "I'm paying for action! Solutions! Movement!"

"Sometimes the best action is inaction," says Pan.

"Huh?" asks Griff.

"Sometimes the best solution is resolution," says Pan, patting his big ham hand.

Griff does a nervous little holding-it-in jig. "And sometimes the best movement is a bowel movement! Whatever you're going to do, do it quick! Things are getting serious in the land down under!" He turns and flounces back into the inn.

Poor little weirdo. Nobody likes him. Nobody talks to him. He just wants to be left alone in the toilet.

I'm talking about Griff. But yeah, I guess the water weirdo, too.

I take another peek down the potty. It must be lonely down there. And then . . . it hits me.

"Maybe we're going about this the wrong way," I suggest.

"Yeah," says Moxie. "Cast something super powerful! What about one of those scrolls Kevin gave you?"

"I only have one left," I tell her. "It's called Stone to String Cheese."

"I can't see that ever coming in handy," mutters Pan, shaking her head.

"You don't know," says Moxie in my defense. "Maybe we'll be starving in a really rocky place. Fart could provide an all-you-can-eat string cheese buffet!"

"We're getting off topic," I say, turning back to the toilet. "What I mean is, maybe we should try using our words instead of our weapons."

"Explain," replies Pan.

"Maybe we should try talking to the water weirdo."

"Interesting," says Pan thoughtfully.

Moxie turns to me. "Can you do that?" she asks. "Can you talk to it?"

I turn to the toilet. And I cast a sweet little spell I've been working on that lets me temporarily talk to any creature. I cast Magic Mouth.

My mom always told me not to talk to weirdos. But this one and I have a nice little chat. Luckily water weirdos are totally reasonable. You just need to find out what they want.

And what this one wants . . . is chicken.

THE INCREDIBLE FART!

MINI MAGIC MAN!

Our client does not seem pleased with our results.

"What do you mean, it's still in there?" roars Griff.

"We made a deal with it," I tell him.

SUPERHEROIC ACHIEVEMENT!

Strike a Bargain with a
Water Weirdo!

(300 Experience Points Awarded)

Griff sighs in defeat. "Fine. What's the deal?"

"It's quite simple," Pan explains. "You feed it one roasted chicken a week, and it agrees to quit biting butts."

We all smile, pleased with our results-oriented approach. "It gets to keep its home and you get to keep your outhouse," I tell him. "It's a fair compromise."

"And if that doesn't work, you could always build another outhouse," Moxie points out. "This place could use another one anyway."

Griff grits his teeth. He grumbles. He gripes. He tells the cook to roast a chicken, and pronto! But he pays us.

SUPERHEROIC ACHIEVEMENT!
Another Satisfied Customer!
(300 Experience Points Awarded)

CHAPTER TWO

The three of us walk heroically down the streets of Conklin, Bizzy buzzing in our wake. We bask in the warm summer sun and the glow of another brave deed accomplished.

Okay, sorting out Griff's toilet troubles isn't exactly on our top-ten list of heroic acts.

Pan, Moxie, and I have been together for quite a while now. Ever since our masters went *POOF!* in a goblin attack gone wrong. Ever since we decided not to return to Krakentop Academy for Heroes. Ever since we set out on our own to become fearless adventurers.

We have braved the Caves of Catastrophe and

emerged triumphant! We have foiled a ruthless pirate captain with nothing but skill, pluck, and an upbeat attitude!! We have fought foul harpies and grimy gurblins and lived to tell the tale boy-oh-boy let me tell you what!!!

Together, we are unbeatable!

Yep, we've become a tight-knit trio. Pan and Moxie and me. They are the ham to my cheese. The hot fudge to my sundae. The tots to my taters.

We even have special hang-out activities. Like every afternoon at one o'clock, Pan and I spar together.

During our last sparring session, we developed this new combo attack. I fire my Magic Missile at a boulder. That breaks off tons of little gravelly

guys. And she monk-manipulates the tiny bits of earth into a deadly barrage of doom! We call it . . .

DEATH BY PEBBLE!

And at least once a week, Moxie and I go window-shopping.

She loves to see the new merchandise at Wynchester's Weapons Emporium. And I love to see the look of longing on her face as she gazes at all the implements of death and destruction. It's our Moxie-and-me bonding time.

Ahhh, the quiet life. Resting. Relaxing. Enjoying the peaceful and tranquil village of Conklin. What could be better?

Seriously, though, I'm losing my marbles. Big-time.

The three of us are staying at the Woozy Wyvern

Inn. And after a month of sharing a room . . . well . . .
I'm starting to miss the monsters.

Moxie leaves everything on the floor. *Everything*.
Her sweaty armor. Her smelly socks. Her *toothbrush*.

And Pan . . . apparently elves are easily grossed out
by human food. Like, if you have a snack, you better
eat it in about 3.5 seconds flat. Because if you don't . . .

Well, you get the idea.

The three of us make a great team. BFFs forever. Buddies for life. All those things.

But crud on a cracker . . . a month of being cooped up together is driving us dopey.

It's time to get out there again. We're ready for excitement! Adventure! A *real* quest.

So that's why we're at the message board in the Conklin town square. It's loaded up with posters and flyers.

Lost dog. Guitar lessons. Babysitter wanted. That kind of stuff.

But also . . . *quests.*

"Very promising," says Pan, tapping her chin thoughtfully. "My mother always said . . . a proper hero needs a proper quest."

"I like that last one," Moxie chimes in. "It comes with a juicy reward!"

We return to our room at the Woozy Wyvern, posters in hand. Ready to make a decision.

But we don't decide anything. We barely make it into our room before a griffin flies through the window. And into my mouth.

Not a full-size griffin. That would be silly. Obviously.

A teeny-tiny griffin. Made out of paper. Obviously.

I spit it onto the floor next to Moxie's socks. And armor. And ponytail holders. And toothbrush.

The griffin flutters back into the air and pecks at my head with a spit-soaked beak. Which is exactly as adorable as it sounds.

"What's this?" Pan asks, snatching the paper griffin. She slowly unfolds it, her eyes scanning the page. "It's a note. From Kevin."

"What's it say?" Moxie asks eagerly.

Pan holds it out. "Read it for yourself."

Hey twerps,

You little dudes did good on my last couple of errands.

Not bad for amateurs.

I've got a new task that needs doing. Just a little jaunt to go and pick up a special item for me.

It's got all the usual stuff. Epic adventure. Sacks of loot.

You know the drill.

Get your butts over to my tower.

Toot sweet. ASAP. Like, yesterday.

Hugs not drugs,

The Great and Powerful Kevin

"Aw, yeah!" says Moxie. "You know what this is?"

"Atrocious penmanship?" asks Pan.

"The cutest magical origami I ever saw?" I suggest.

"Nope," says Moxie with a grin. "This . . . is a quest!"

Pan flops down dejectedly on her perfectly made bed and holds up the three posters. "So are these."

"Well, sure," says Moxie. "But this says there'll be 'sacks of loot.' Plus it's Kevin!"

"Exactly," moans Pan.

Moxie flops next to her. "What's the problem? We always come back from Kevin's quests with pouches bulging with gold!"

"It's true," Pan concedes. "They are often profitable."

"And they're always exciting," I chime in. "I mean, we practically died on the last one! How's that for exciting?"

"You are right," she nods.

"So?" asks Moxie.

Pan walks to the window and stares out at the rooftops of Conklin. Moxie and I give her a moment. We know Pan well enough to wait her out. To give her a second to center herself with the universe. Or whatever.

Finally she turns back to us, her expression grim.

"I crave more noble exploits!" she cries. "If we truly

are heroes, shouldn't we be helping people? Regardless of the reward?"

"We *have been* helping people," I point out. "Being able to take a dump without getting bit in the butt by a water weirdo? *Super* helpful!"

"I want to be proper heroes on a proper quest," Pan says, shaking the posters at us. "Wouldn't you rather aid a noble knight? Or rescue a kidnapped prince? Or capture a no-good thief?"

"Well, sure," says Moxie. "But Kevin—"

Pan tilts her head. "I do not trust Kevin. What is he doing with these items that we have brought him?" she cries, almost to herself. "The fart of a lamia? The barf of a bedazzler?" She sighs. "My heart tells me that we would be wise to stay as far away from him as possible. And yet . . ."

Silence. She turns back to the window.

"And yet?" prompts Moxie.

Pan draws a breath and toys absently with her necklace. "And yet, once again, we find ourselves drawn to his tower. As if something calls to us."

"Duh," I say, snatching the note. "*Kevin* calls to us. Offering an adventurous quest. And sacks of loot. And let's be honest, we could use the money."

"I know," says Pan. "Our funds are almost depleted. But . . ."

Moxie walks over to Pan. "Look, Pan. We trust your instincts, okay? But what if we just go and see what his quest is all about?"

"Sure!" I say. "Just hear him out. No commitment."

"Exactly," says Moxie. "All three of us have to agree. If we like the quest, we'll take it! We'll get a nice fat payday and then we can do any noble quest you want."

I hold Pan's bo staff out to her. "What do you think?"

Pan tucks her necklace under her tunic. She takes the note, her nimble fingers folding it back into the griffin. As if in response to its renewed shape, the griffin flutters before her, alive once again.

"It is a lovely griffin," she says.

She grabs her bo staff from me. "All right. We'll do it. On one condition."

I get nervous. "What's that?"

She cocks a pointy eyebrow at me and smirks. "That you take a bath before we go. You smell like you've had your head stuck in a toilet all morning."

CHAPTER THREE

Kevin's tower looms before us in hazy morning sunlight like a bloody spear. Promising all kinds of cool things. Adventure. Excitement. A horrible grisly death.

Well, at least we're out of the house.

I'm just about to knock on the door when I hear it.

Kevin's mom. Yelling. Again.

"NOW!" she howls. "MAKE IT NOW!"

I cringe at the sound of her voice. This lady is constantly wailing at the poor guy like a banshee.

"I can't make it yet!" The voice of Kevin. "Would you get off my back?!"

I'm glad she's not my mom. And I'm glad she stays

tucked away in her hidey-hole upstairs. I have no desire to come face-to-face with this lady.

"MAKE IT NOW!" she cries again, setting my teeth on edge. "THE TIME HAS COME!"

"The time has not even come," he yells back. "Quit being so pushy! I need the third ingredient!"

Our ears perk up.

I know it's not polite to stand on the front porch and eavesdrop on private conversations between a wizard and his squawky mama. But this is just too good.

"YOU NEVER DO ANYTHING RIGHT!" she yells. "GET IT! GET IT NOW!"

"I'm working on it! GEEZ!" cries Kevin. "Look, we have the lamia fart. And we have the bedazzler barf."

Lamia fart. Bedazzler barf. We are intimately familiar with those items. We got them for Kevin on our previous quests.

"I just need thing number three," Kevin continues. "And then we'll be ready. Okay? GOSH!"

"AND THEN . . . WE WILL BURN TOLIVAR!" cries the old lady. "WE WILL BURN VERBINA!"

"Yeah, yeah," comes Kevin's exhausted voice. "We'll make a nice tolivar-verbena bonfire. Until then just chill out! Okay?"

Moxie giggles uncomfortably. "What's thing number three?" she whispers.

"I dunno," I answer.

"What's tolivar?" she asks. "What's verbena?"

Pan tucks her hair behind her ear thoughtfully. "Verbena is an herb known among the elves for its healing properties," she explains. "Perhaps tolivar is a plant as well."

"Maybe." Moxie taps the end of her hammer. "If Kevin's gonna burn some herbs, maybe he's cooking up something for his mom. Like an ointment for the old lady's arthritis!" She giggles.

"Or a denture cream," I add, snickering.

"Or a wrinkle reducer!" Moxie whispers with a laugh.

"Or something more sinister," Pan hisses ominously.

Moxie turns skeptically toward Pan. "Kevin?" She snorts out a laugh. "How sinister can he be? The guy can't even get his own lamia farts!"

"Be that as it may, if Kevin is using the items we got him for nefarious means, then we are partly responsible for the outcome," says Pan grimly. "We acquired them, after all."

Gosh. I never thought about that. Also I'm not 100 percent sure what "nefarious" means. But it doesn't sound good.

The yelling continues. Our attention turns back to the door.

"Just take a chill pill!" Kevin yells. "I've got some heroes coming."

I raise my eyebrows at Moxie and Pan. Heroes. They're talking about us.

Cool.

"They'll go to Glacierbane and get our third item," says Kevin. "But it's gonna be risky."

The woman's voice fills with an intensity that sends my skin crawling for cover. "LET THEM RISK IT ALL! LET THEM DIE! I MUST HAVE RELIEF FROM THIS TORMENT!"

I raise my eyebrows at Moxie and Pan. Dying. They're talking about us.

Not cool.

Pan pulls us away.

"I do not like this," she whispers. "They seem very willing to risk our lives."

Moxie shrugs. "So what else is new?"

But I can tell from her face. Pan is not convinced.

"Look, I'm not gonna lie, his old lady sounds like a piece of work," Moxie concedes. "But there's no harm in hearing him out, is there? If you've still got a skeevy feeling after that, then we're done."

"You promise?" says Pan.

"Of course," says Moxie.

I put my arm on Pan's shoulder. "We do things together or not at all."

Pan looks like she's about to say something heartfelt.

But she never gets a chance. Because at that moment, the front door bursts open.

It's Kevin.

And he's got peanut butter on his forehead. Don't ask me why.

CHAPTER FOUR

Kevin eyeballs us suspiciously. Nervously. Like maybe we've heard too much. "Hey, you knuckleheads. How long have you been standing there?"

Moxie shrugs innocently. "We just got here. Why?"

"No reason," he says. "Took you long enough, that's all. So you ready to hear about this sweet quest, or what?"

Moxie and I look to Pan. She shoots us a smirk and walks past Kevin into the tower. "Your note made it sound exciting," she says casually. "Let's hear it."

We follow her in, and Kevin closes the door behind us.

"Friends!" cries a voice. There's a blur of blue skin, orange eyes, and clanking tools.

TickTock!
Phibling Gizmo Whiz!

The little phibling hugs with a ferocity that belies his small size. TickTock has saved our butts more times than we can count. But our reunion is cut short.

"Step aside, TickTock," Kevin says gruffly. "These guys are here on official hero business."

Kevin leads us past the staircase and into the entry hall. "If you think you loved your quest for the bedazzler barf, wait till you hear this one. I've got one word for you." He spreads his arms dramatically. "Glacierbane!"

"That technically sounds like two words," Pan points out, wandering around the foyer. "Not one."

Kevin deflates. "You wanna hear about my cool quest or not?"

"Let's hear it!" Moxie cries, gripping and ungripping her hammer. "I don't know what a glacierbane is, but it sounds amazing already!"

But something Pan said has stuck with me. *If Kevin*

26

is using the items we got him for nefarious means, then we are partly responsible for the outcome. And she's right.

I decide it's time for some answers. "First things first," I say. "What are you doing with the stuff we bring you?"

"Huh?" Kevin is taken aback.

"The lamia fart," I say. "The bedazzler barf. Whatever this third thing is you want us to get. What are you doing with them?"

He cracks his knuckles in annoyance. "None of your beeswax."

I take a deep breath, mustering my nerve. "Not good enough," I say.

Moxie nods, following my lead. "Yeah," she joins in. "If we're getting this stuff for you, we deserve to know what you're doing with it."

TickTock watches us wide-eyed.

Kevin smacks his forehead. "Look, don't trouble your pretty little selves about things you don't understand." He puffs himself up. "I am a mysterious sorcerer! The greatest magical mind of my time!"

It would be a lot easier to take him seriously if he didn't have peanut butter smeared into his hair. "I am exploring the inner workings of the very fabric of time and space!" he cries, warming to the subject. "And if I need odd little ingredients to do my magic-making, well, whoop-de-do! But that's nothing for you little runts to worry about . . . HEY!"

His "HEY" is directed at Pan. Who has been wandering casually around the foyer. And casually up the stairs. To the second floor.

"NO!" Kevin roars. "BAD ELF! THOSE STAIRS ARE OFF-LIMITS! NOT EVEN TICKTOCK IS ALLOWED UP THERE!"

Pan turns slowly, her eyebrows raised, her fingers fiddling absently with her necklace. She stands boldly in the face of Kevin's rage. "Please answer the question," she says. "What do you need these items for?"

He marches toward her. "Get off those stairs, kid. I'm not joking." And for the first time since I've known him, there is danger in his tone.

Pan descends the stairs. "It's cold up there," she says, shivering.

"What can I say?" he retorts. "The heat is broken." He turns to the three of us with a forced smile. "Now. Do you rugrats want to hear about my quest or not?"

"No," says Pan, arms crossed. "Thank you for the offer. But we decline."

Kevin chuckles. "Come off it. You know my quests are always awesome!"

"Be that as it may," Pan says firmly. "We'll pass."

Kevin blinks. "You're serious?" His eyes dart to Moxie and me. "You guys too?"

Moxie and I step up behind Pan. "She speaks for all of us," says Moxie. "We do things together or not at all."

The wizard huffs impatiently. "Did I make it clear to you losers that I'm offering primo cash for this one?"

Pan calmly walks toward the front door, Moxie and me on her heels. "We appreciate all the opportunities you've given us in the past," she says. "But you simply have too many secrets for our comfort. Nothing you offer us will compel us to take this quest."

There is only silence behind us. Then Kevin's hushed voice . . .

"Oh, yeah?" He cracks his neck. "What if I could let you see your mother one last time? *Panalathalasas?*"

Crud on a cracker.

Pan stops dead. Her face has gone ghostly white.

She turns slowly, her bottom lip quivering. Her voice catches in her throat. "How?" she asks. "How do you know about my mother?"

Kevin leans against the banister, picking dirt from his fingernails. "Let's just say I am great," he says.

"How do you know my elvish name?" asks Pan.

Kevin smooths back his mussed hair. "Let's just say I am powerful," he says.

"My mother is dead," Pan chokes out. "How could you possibly let me see her again?"

He crosses his arms and looks up, his eyes piercing into hers. "Let's just say I am . . . Kevin," he says. "And I have my ways."

"Look, Kev," says Moxie, placing a hand protectively on Pan's shoulder. "She said we're not interested. And she's not going to be tempted by your promises of—"

"We'll do it," Pan says.

Kevin chuckles softly. "You don't even know what the quest is."

Pan swallows. "Whatever it is," she whispers. "We'll do it."

CHAPTER FIVE

A smug smile spreads across Kevin's bearded face. He knows he's got us.

"Pan . . ." I start, reaching out to my friend.

"No," she says, pulling away.

"Pan, are you . . . ?" begins Moxie.

"Not now," she says. Her face is stone. Pinched. Tight. I can't imagine what she's feeling at this moment.

Kevin shoots us once last triumphant look, then turns and leads us toward the back of the tower. "Okay, kiddos," he shoots over his shoulder. "Follow me."

The wizard takes us down a hall, through an archway, and up a long spiral staircase. TickTock trails nervously behind us. By the time we reach the top of the stairs, I'm panting like an exhausted owlbear.

We emerge into a dark round room. In the dim lighting I can just make out some kind of large tube-shaped contraption in the center of the room.

"Hold on to your nunchucks," says Kevin. He nods to TickTock, and the phibling pulls a series of levers. I feel the floor shake. I hear the grinding of chains. And the whole room starts to rise.

Up, up, up we go. Moxie plants her feet solidly, and I grab on to her for support. Suddenly the room floods with blinding light. The roof of Kevin's tower has opened up like a clamshell, and we've risen right out the top, into the sunlight.

Our teetering platform grinds to a halt high above

the tower. A hawk soars past us, wondering what the heck we're doing way up here. I'm wondering that myself.

"Welcome to my observatory," Kevin says proudly.

"Whoa," says Moxie in awe.

Whoa is right.

"The view is magnificent," says Pan softly. "But what does this have to do with your quest?"

"Well, I didn't bring you all the way up here just for the breathtaking scenery and the fresh air," Kevin says sarcastically.

He walks over to the tube-shaped gizmo. I can see now . . . it's some sort of giant telescope.

Kevin flips some switches and rotates a crank on his enormous contraption. The whole thing swivels. Pointing its big eye toward Conklin. Past Conklin. To the north. "Take a look."

We each peek through the viewfinder. A mountain range zooms into view. Snowcapped cliffs. Rocky, craggy bluffs. And climbing past it all, a single peak disappears into a fog of clouds.

Kevin waves grandly toward the horizon. "Those," he says, "are the Frostflung Mountains. Loaded to the brim with all kinds of monstrous tundra-loving nasties. Be especially mindful of the froblins."

"Froblins?" asks Moxie.

"Frost goblins," Kevin explains. "Foul critters."

"Lovely," says Pan coldly.

"At the top of the highest peak, among all the snowballs and icicles, is Glacierbane." Kevin wiggles

FROBLIN

Frost goblin.

Foul critters.

his fingers theatrically. He cocks his eyebrows at us, extremely impressed with himself.

"You're going to make us ask?" I say.

"Yep," he says smugly.

"Why?" I say.

"Dramatic effect."

I really want to push him off this tower. I sigh in defeat. "Fine. What is a glacierbane?"

"Not a what," he says. "A who. Glacierbane . . . is a dragon."

Silence settles over us for a moment. But it doesn't last long. Moxie is already pulling out her favorite book . . . *Buzzlock's Big Book of Beasts*.

"Have you lost your shaggy peanut-butter-crusted mind?" she cries, flipping pages. "We can't slay a dragon!"

DRAGON

Deadly breath.

Ferocious claws.

Terrible teeth.

Lots of treasure.

Don't even think about slaying one.

"You knuckleheads," says Kevin. "Always jumping to the wrong conclusion. I never said *slay*."

"Then what?" asks Pan.

"Steal from!" Kevin exclaims.

"You want us to steal treasure from a dragon?" I ask.

"What? No!" cries Kevin. "Any idiot knows you don't lay a finger on a dragon's treasure! Sheesh!"

"Why not?" asks Moxie, studying her book. "There's a lot of gold in this picture. That dragon wouldn't miss it if we took a little."

"Hordewrath! That's why not!" roars Kevin.

"Hordewrath?" asks Pan.

Kevin sighs loudly. "Look, dragons possess a special little trait known as hordewrath. They instinctively know every bit of their treasure. Down to the last gold coin and sparkly ruby. If you touch even one tiny piece, that beast will sense it instantly."

"And if that happens?" I ask.

"Oh, I dunno," muses Kevin. "IT'LL BRING WRATH AND RUIN DOWN UPON YOU ALL!"

Moxie gulps. Pan gulps. TickTock gulps. I gulp. Gulping all around.

Got it. No touchy the treasure.

"Then what?" asks Pan impatiently. "What do you want us to take from the dragon?"

"Something he'll never miss," says Kevin, enjoying the moment.

"What?" cries Pan in frustration. "Spit it out already!"

Kevin lowers his voice to a mysterious whisper. "You enter that dragon's lair . . ."

"Yeah?" I say.

". . . and you find . . ."

"Yeah?" says Moxie.

". . . the dragon's . . ."

"Yes?" says Pan.

". . . dookie."

We let it sink in.

"As in dung?" Moxie asks.

"As in poo?" I ask.

"As in doo-doo?" Moxie asks.

"As in caca?" I ask.

"Yes!" Kevin crows. "It's the perfect heist! The dragon will never miss it! See, a dragon eats a lot of people. Idiots lured by all that loot who think they can slay this big mean lizard. Which means it swallows a lot of people. People wearing stuff. Magic stuff. Magic armor. Magic rings. Magic swords. Magic necklaces."

"If you're looking for a magic item, there must be an easier way," says Pan.

"Yeah," I cry, reaching into my robes. "I've got a scroll of Stone to String Cheese right here! You can have it!"

"Doofus!" cries Kevin. "I don't want your stupid string cheese scroll!"

"Told you," whispers Pan. "It's a worthless spell."

"Focus, people!" roars Kevin. "I need a magic item from a pile of dragon poop!" He shakes his head impatiently and pulls down a little chart from the side of the telescope.

"Look. When a magic item passes through a dragon's digestive system, it changes. It gets . . . somehow . . . supercharged into an artifact of immense power. Don't ask me how it works. Something to do with enzymes. It goes in this end *normal* magic . . . and gets pooped out of this end *super-duper* magic."

"Whoa," says Moxie. "That's cool."

"Yes," agrees Kevin. "It's very cool. And I need it."

"So . . . poo?" Pan says, shaking her head in disbelief.

"This is our noble quest? You want us to dig through poo."

"Now you got it, sister!" cries Kevin happily.

We got it. I'm just not sure we want it.

"Heroes will need good sneaking," TickTock points out quietly. His orange eyes stare up at us determinedly. "TickTock will go with."

"Not gonna happen!" says Kevin firmly. "No way!

Too dangerous! I'm not letting you guys break my phibling."

"Not Kevin's phibling," TickTock snaps. I hear annoyance in his voice for the first time ever. "TickTock is TickTock's phibling. And TickTock is going with!"

"Sheesh. Fine." The wizard turns back to us with a stern look. "But you dweebs just remember: Whatever you do, DON'T TOUCH THE DRAGON'S TREASURE! OR YOU'RE ALL DEAD! Doody, yes! Booty, no!"

He turns to Pan, a shrewd look in his beady eyes. "You do this and you get to say a proper goodbye to dear old Mommy."

TickTock clears his throat. "Kevin was having the power to do this thing for elf-girl before now?" he asks quizzically. "And he never offered to do it?"

Kevin seems surprised by the phibling's words. "Maybe!" he sputters. "Possibly! Conceivably! Quit helping, TickTock!" He turns back to us. "It never came up, okay?! But it's on the table now."

"So you're blackmailing us," says Moxie defensively.

"Please!" cries Kevin. "This isn't blackmail. It's a very persuasive job offer."

"Call it what you want," I chime in. "A real friend would let Pan see her mom anyway."

Kevin chuckles. "You kids crack me up. We aren't *friends*. This is business. You give me something I want, and I give you something you want. That's how this works. And right now I want you to dig through a big pile of dragon caca and bring me back whatever's inside it."

"Fine," says Pan tightly. "But after this, our business is concluded. For good."

"Fine," says Kevin with a sniff.

TickTock steps forward, wringing his hands. "That is going for TickTock, too."

"TickTock?" says Kevin in surprise. He scowls at us. "Now see what you've done?" he snarls. "You've upset my phibling."

"NOT YOUR PHIBLING!" cries TickTock.

Kevin throws an arm around the phibling. "Buddy. Pal. Chum. How can you say that after all we've been through together?"

TickTock pulls away from Kevin's grasp. The phibling stands straight and tall, all two feet of him. "TickTock is not liking how Kevin is treating TickTock's friends."

Kevin stares at the phibling. His eyes roam over each of us slowly. Perhaps TickTock has gotten through to Kevin's humanity. Perhaps his words have broken through Kevin's hard outer shell to the soft nougaty center that I suspect is really in there. Perhaps . . .

"You know what?" says Kevin quietly. "Fine. Just get me my item. After that, I don't care if I see you guys ever again."

He darts a cold eye at TickTock. "Any of you."

CHAPTER SIX

It's a quiet walk back to Conklin.

Pan is withdrawn, lost in her own thoughts. Same with TickTock.

I can tell Moxie wants to talk about things. But she stays silent. We all do.

The next morning, we pack our stuff into Bizzy's cart. Pan slips off to Merchant Mike's Sell-All Shop and returns with a bundle of supplies. Food, water, and some snazzy winter coats.

It's good thinking. After all, we're going to a place called Frostflung. You don't put the word "frost" in the name unless it's pretty chilly there.

I rig my giant bee to the cart. As we ride out of

Conklin and leave the Woozy Wyvern Inn behind, I realize the cart contains everything we own. Who knows when we'll be back home. Or *if* we'll be back home.

We steer north. Toward the Frostflung Mountains.

Toward Glacierbane the dragon.

Toward a big old pile of poo with our names written all over it.

TickTock sits in the back of the cart, tinkering on some mechanical gizmo. A little metal man.

We're an hour outside of Conklin when I finally lean over to Pan and ask the question. The question that I know Moxie and I are both wondering.

"Pan?" I ask softly. "What happened to your mom?"

Pan takes a slow, deep breath. She looks at me sadly and smiles. "I'm not ready to talk about it," she says. "When I am, you and Moxie will be the first to know."

That's fair. I know Pan well enough to wait her out.

Give her space. Let her become one with the cosmos. Or whatever.

We ride for two days. We pass farmers and merchants heading to Conklin to sell their stuff. Moxie and I chit-chat, but Pan just stares into the distance, lost in her own thoughts.

It's late afternoon on the third day when Pan finally speaks. "It's time to leave the road," she says.

She's right.

The road goes west. But our way is north. Into the wilderness.

"I'm sorry I got us into this," Pan says, breaking the bleak silence. "Going to a dragon's lair is crazy, I know. But I had to say yes."

Moxie grins. "Don't be silly," she says. "Sounds like fun!"

"Yeah," I jump in. "If you hadn't said yes, I would have said yes for you."

"TickTock is thirding that," the phibling says from the back.

Pan flashes a small grateful smile.

She stares out over the rocky wilderness spread before us.

"Kevin said he would let me see my mother one last time." Pan's eyes search ours. "Do you really think he can do that?"

Moxie and I remain silent. We have no answers.

But TickTock lays his tools down and climbs to the front of the cart. "TickTock is not knowing about magic," he says with a shrug. "But TickTock is knowing this: Kevin is keeping lots of secrets. But Kevin is not a liar."

He turns his bulbous orange eyes to Pan's delicate ones. "TickTock thinks that if the Kevin is saying he can do this thing . . . then the Kevin can do it."

Pan lays a hand on the phibling's shoulder. "I'm sorry I got you fired, TickTock."

"Silly elf-girl," TickTock says with a gurgly laugh. "Elf-girl did not get TickTock fired. TickTock decided."

He looks back at his bundle of tools and gizmos. "TickTock will miss having his own workshop," he says sadly. Then he turns and smiles at us. "But TickTock is not sorry. Friends are being more important than workshops."

We pass under a huge stone arch, curtains of dangling moss hanging high overhead, dripping frosty droplets of evening dew down on us.

But Pan is oblivious to the drip-drops. She looks at us like she wants desperately to say something deep and profound.

But she doesn't. Instead she does something completely un-Pan-like.

She stands up and pulls all three of us into a crushing hug.

Good thing too. Because at that moment, a spear buries itself into the wooden seat right where she was sitting.

We are under attack.

By shroomies.

CHAPTER SEVEN

Leave it to shroomies to ruin the moment.

"Ambush!" cries Moxie. "Don't look now, guys. But there are fungus among us." She leaps off the cart, hammer in hand.

Dozens of the little fungi fiends come charging out from behind the arch. But I'm not worried. After all . . . they're *mushrooms*. And *we* are mighty heroes.

Moxie and Pan twirl their weapons, hammer and bo staff sending the shroomies flying.

TickTock springs at the attacking toadstools with his dagger, slicing and dicing like a short-order cook during the dinner rush.

I leap forward to untether Bizzy from the cart and give her a fighting chance. Then I turn to unleash my magic on these tiny appetizers.

"Pew-pew-patchoo!" Flaming darts fly from my hands, sending two attacking shroomies into the dirt.

The battle is on.

Bizzy stings right and left, but her pointy butt of doom has no effect on these little mushroom men. Several of them leap up, grab her legs, and start pulling her to the ground.

"Get out of there, Bizzy!" I cry.

Moxie spins in a circle, knocking Bizzy's attackers senseless.

Pan is a flurry of fists and feet. She sends a handful of the freaky fungi into the dirt.

But more just fill in to take their place.

Bizzy hovers out of reach overhead, dodging spears, helpless to defend us against the rushing mob.

"Pew-pew-patchoo!" I unleash another barrage of flaming arrows. The force of my magic knocks me off-balance, sending me into the dirt.

Seeing me flat on my crack, a shroomie lets out a cry of rage and leaps at me, its small spear aimed at my heart.

I love that spell. Good old Gas Attack.

"Fart!" cries Pan. "Death by Pebble!"

Got it. I shoot Magic Missiles into the stone archway, littering the air with bits of stone. Pan sends the gravelly barrage shooting toward the shroomies, putting several out of business for good.

But at least two dozen shroom dudes continue the attack. We are badly outnumbered.

"There are too many!" cries Pan.

"TickTock is getting shish-kebabed by shroomies!" yells the phibling, waving his dagger.

"Get to the cart!" Moxie yells over the din.

"What's wrong with these mushrooms?" I cry. "Don't they know that we are mighty heroes?!"

I turn to run, flinging a spell over my shoulder to slow the shroomies down: *"Plantainitar au musa!"*

WHAT ACTUALLY HAPPENED...

1. I'm not watching where I'm going.

2. I slam into Moxie's back.

SLAM

3. Banana peels explode into the air all around us.

4. The four of us slip. We slide. We stumble. We fall to the floor.

5. The shroomies surround us, jabbing with their pokey sticks.

PS—No victory parade.

Great. Thanks to me, we are about to be skewered by an unruly mob of pizza toppings.

How humiliating.

But suddenly the sound of galloping fills my ears.

There's the thrum of a bowstring. The flash of steel arrowheads. Several of the closest mushroom monsters tumble to the dust.

A tall hooded figure dashes past. Wearing fancy armor. Gripping an ornate bow. Firing an onslaught of arrows at our attackers.

And riding . . . a unicorn.

It happens so fast, the remaining mushrooms don't even notice. They keep poking and prodding at us. Moxie fends them off with her shield, but she won't hold out forever.

The rider spurs the unicorn to a gallop. With rapid-fire fingers, the mysterious stranger circles us, putting an arrow into the cap of every remaining shroomie.

Their angry little eyes blink in disbelief. And then they flop to the ground.

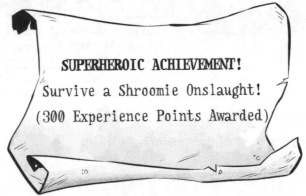

SUPERHEROIC ACHIEVEMENT!
Survive a Shroomie Onslaught!
(300 Experience Points Awarded)

The unicorn rears up with a victorious whinny, tossing its silky mane regally in the wind. The fading sunlight gleams off the rider's golden armor.

There's no doubt. We are in the presence of greatness.

"Wow," says Pan, leaping to her feet.

"Wow is right!" Moxie cries.

I pull myself up, brushing banana from my robes. "Thanks for the help, mister," I call out.

In a flash, the bowstring is pulled taut, arrow aimed at my heart. Golden-green eyes glare down at me from the depths of the hood.

I take a moment to let my life pass before my eyes. The early stuff is kinda boring, but the ending picks up nicely. Which is great, since it seems like it's gonna be the last thing I ever see.

But the rider relaxes the bowstring.

A tattooed hand sweeps back the hood, revealing a head of spiky pink hair.

"You're welcome," the rider says, cocking an eyebrow at us. "But I am no mister."

CHAPTER EIGHT

"Whoa," whispers Moxie.

"Whoa," whispers Pan.

Whoa is right.

The rider pulls her fingers through her short pink hair. She's older than us. Maybe sixteen or so. Human.

"Crud on a cracker," I say. "Sorry about that, miss. I mean ma'am. I mean madam." I gulp nervously.

"No worries, Little Wiz," she says. She leaps from her mount with a grin.

"Wow!" says Moxie, running to her. "Where did you get that wicked bow?!"

The girl holds up her bow for us to admire. "Acquired it from a mountain troll's stash." She looks Moxie over. "You're packing some heat yourself there, sis. Nice hammer."

Moxie beams proudly and holds her weapon aloft. "Solid silver. Got it in the underwater lair of a lich."

The girl nods. "Fierce."

"I have to say," Pan says with admiration. "I have never seen a human nock an arrow with such speed. You have elf-like reflexes."

The girl sizes Pan up. "You look like you're pretty quick on the draw yourself."

Pan flushes at the unexpected praise.

The girl tosses her cape back, revealing a golden rose emblazoned across her armor.

"Wait a minute!" cries Moxie. "I know who you are!"

"Um . . . you do?" asks the girl.

"Fart!" Moxie thrusts out her hand. "Gimme those wanted posters. From Conklin!"

The girl slowly nocks an arrow to her bowstring as I pull the roll of posters from my pocket. Moxie starts shuffling through them.

The wanted poster for the thief . . .

The flyer about the kidnapped prince . . .

And then she finds the one she's after.

The noble knight . . . in search of helpers to aid in a quest.

"This is you!" she cries to Seraphim, holding up the poster. "You're a Knight of the Rose!"

I grab the poster and inspect it closely. She's right. The armor is the same.

TWANG!

The girl's arrow rips the posters from my fingertips, pinning them to the side of our cart. A quirky smile washes across her face. "Bull's-eye," she says. "You got me."

She shoulders her bow. "Allow me to introduce myself," she says. "I'm Seraphim the—"

"The Knight of the Rose!" says TickTock excitedly.

"Well, I don't think we need any fancy nicknames," says the knight. "Just Seraphim is fine."

"Wow! A real knight!" says Moxie. "I never knew a knight could use a bow. I thought knights only used swords and lances and stuff like that."

Seraphim shrugs. "Well, we all have our special skills, don't we? We work with what we've got."

Moxie rushes forward and grabs the girl's hand. "I'm Moxie Battleborne. This is TickTock the phibling." Tick-Tock waves shyly. "This giant bug is Bizzy," says Moxie, rubbing Bizzy's bumbly belly.

"The little wiz is Fart," says Pan with an eyebrow quirked at me.

"Sorry," says the knight. "Did you say *Fart*?"

"Long story," says Moxie with a giggle.

"And I am Pan Silversnow." Pan offers the knight a respectful bow. The girl returns it solemnly.

Seraphim waves a hand at the creature beside her. "This is my faithful companion," she says. "Sparkles."

The unicorn tosses its mane. It stomps its hooves. It whinnies in greeting.

And then . . . it speaks. "That's spelled with a star instead of an *a*, okay?" it says. "And super-curvy writing. Like **Sp☆rkles**."

"Whoa!" I cry. "A talking unicorn!"

"Oh. My. Gosh. Did you just call me . . . A UNICORN?" Sparkles says, tossing her mane dramatically.

I see now that instead of a horn protruding from the creature's head, there is a long silver spoon. Which is weird, I'm not gonna lie.

"Can you even believe this guy, Sera?" the animal says with a sniff.

Seraphim laughs. "Calm your hooves, Sparkles. Little Wiz didn't mean anything by it."

"Little Wiz?" says Sparkles, eyeing the pile of banana peels around us. "More like Banana Boy. Am I right? Did you see that fruit salad come flying out of his hands? That was comedy gold!"

I feel my face flush red. But Seraphim turns to us with a wink. "Don't worry about Sparkles. She gets sorta touchy about people calling her a unicorn. You see, Sparkles . . . is a spoonicorn."

"That's right," mutters Sparkles. "And I'm not touchy. I'm, like, totally *passionate*."

"Oh my gosh," Moxie cries in excitement, yanking out Buzzlock's book. "A real and actual spoonicorn!"

SPOONICORN

Distant cousin of the unicorn.

Single magical spoon instead of a horn.

Producer of tasty treats.

See also *balloonicorn* and *bassoonicorn.*

"It is fortunate for us that you two showed up when you did," says Pan.

"For real!" says Moxie, snapping her book closed. "You saved our heinies from those shroomies."

I huff in exasperation. "Let's not get carried away. I still had some magic up my sleeves."

"Totally!" says Sparkles. "You were probably just about to conjure up some super-ferocious pineapples. Or maybe an ominous fig. Am I right?"

I'm not so sure I like this spoonicorn.

"It was no biggie," says Seraphim. "We just lent a helping hand." Her glinting green eyes pass over Moxie's battle-scarred shield. Pan's well-used bo staff. "Judging by those weapons, you ladies have seen scarier action than shroomies."

Moxie puffs with pride.

"Speaking of shroomies . . ." Seraphim saunters over to the nearest one. She plunges her fist into the fleshy cap on the creature's head and feels around. "These guys have buried treasure in their squishy little noggins."

SQUELCH!

She yanks her hand out and holds up a gleaming nugget. "Shroomie sporepod. These baubles will fetch a fat prize."

"Whoa! There's one of those in every shroomie?" Moxie asks excitedly. "We're rich!" She dives toward the vanquished fungi and is soon armpit-deep in shroomie noggins.

In a matter of minutes, we have a fat pile of spore-pods glinting gold in the sunset.

"Ew. That's narsty." Sparkles gags. "They still have goo on them." But Seraphim just laughs.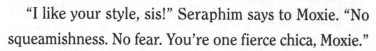

"I like your style, sis!" Seraphim says to Moxie. "No squeamishness. No fear. You're one fierce chica, Moxie."

Moxie beams at the praise and starts dividing the sporepods into five portions.

Seraphim gathers up her share. "Nice," she says with a satisfied grin. "These will fatten up some very hungry orphans."

This stops Moxie cold. "Wait. Orphans? You're going to give them to orphans?"

"Oh my gosh! Yes!" says Sparkles. "Orphans!"

Seraphim shrugs. "Well, and other assorted poor people. Farmers, peasants. Like that."

"Poor people?" I look down at the small pile of golden sporepods before me. "You donate to farmers?"

"Oh my gosh! Yes!" says Sparkles. "Farmers!"

"But hey, don't forget," says Seraphim. "The spirit needs to be fed as well as the body. So I always like to give a little offering to the monks over at the Grayraven monastery."

Pan gasps softly. "Did you say . . . ?"

"Oh my gosh! Yes!" says Sparkles. "Monkeys!"

The three of us look at one another. We look down at our piles of golden sporepods. And we act as one.

"Take mine!" says Moxie. "For the orphans!"

"The farmers need all the help they can get!" I shove my sporepods at the knight.

"The good monks at the monastery will benefit from these far more than I," says Pan, placing her portion at Seraphim's feet with a bow.

Seraphim's jaw drops. "You guys! No way! You earned those." She shoves the pile back at us.

Pan holds up her hand. "We insist."

Seraphim just looks at us in silence. She seems to be at a loss for words. Finally she scoops up the pile and tucks it into the spoonicorn's saddlebags.

She turns, emotion misting her eyes. "Wow. Just wow. Orphans across the realms will eat better because of Moxie Battleborne, Pan Silversnow, and the Fart."

The spoonicorn snorts at the mention of my name. But Seraphim, Knight of the Rose, beams down at us. "Noble names for noble heroes."

We bask in the glow of the knight's praise. One by one, our eyes turn to TickTock.

The phibling stares at us. He fingers his sporepods nervously. And he starts shoving them in his backpack.

"Don't look at TickTock," he says. "TickTock just lost his job. Is saving for a new workshop."

"HAHAHAHAHA!" The spoonicorn snorts with unbridled laughter. "Oh my gosh! I can't even. I love this phibling!"

CHAPTER NINE

We make camp and feast on roasted shroomies.

I don't normally like veggies. But I have to admit, they taste better when you slay them yourself.

"Moxie, I completely love your armor," says Sparkles. *"Très jolie!* That's 'super cute' in Elvish, by the way."

Pan smirks. "That's not Elvish."

"Well, whatever," says Sparkles. "It's still super cute!"

"Gosh!" says Moxie. "Thanks! This chestplate was custom-made!"

The spoonicorn nods in approval. "Thought so. Classic lines. Understated with just a touch of glam influence. And Pan," she says, turning to the elf, "the embroidery on your monk robes is primo stuff. So chic."

Pan smiles and bows her thanks.

I glance down at my own robes.

I admit . . . they haven't had a good cleaning since we trudged through the swamps of Blight Bog Funk. Or since we dug around in the water weirdo's toilet.

Or since . . . ever.

Seraphim's golden armor glints fiercely in the fading sunset. Next to her, my robes look like a thrift-store granny dress. I suddenly feel underdressed. Embarrassed. Frumpy, even.

I wrap my robes around me self-consciously.

Thankfully, Moxie steers the conversation away from fashion. "So, Seraphim," she says, leaning eagerly toward the knight. "What are you and Sparkles doing out here?"

"Well . . ." Seraphim stands and stretches. She runs her fingers through her shock of pink hair and walks over to my wanted posters still pinned to the cart.

She grabs the posters and flips through them until she finds the one she's after. "We're on a noble quest. Rescue mission," she says proudly, holding up the flyer. "Kidnapped prince."

Sparkles tosses her mane. "That's right. And I bet he's a total cutie patootie. Princes always are."

Seraphim rolls her eyes and grins. "Not that we're interested in that."

"Speak for yourself!" cries Sparkles.

"A proper hero," says Pan wistfully. "On a proper quest."

"Yeah!" says Moxie. "Fierce!"

Seraphim rolls up the posters. She starts to tuck them into her belt, but I reach out, and she returns them to me.

"How about you guys?" Seraphim says, grabbing a

stick and poking the fire. "What brings you into these fungi-infested wastelands?"

"We are doing a quest also," chimes in TickTock.

"Not just any quest!" I point out. "We're going into . . . wait for it . . . a dragon's lair."

Seraphim's eyes widen. "Wow. A dragon's lair. Impressive." She cracks her neck, deep in thought. "What tempts you enough to go in there? Rivers of gold? Mountains of emeralds? Piles of rubies and silver?"

"Well, sure, there's probably loads of treasure," says Moxie.

"Yeah, but we can't touch the stuff," I remind Moxie. "'Cuz of hordewrath."

The knight nods her head vaguely. "Sure, sure. Hordewrath." She seems lost in thought.

I slip the posters under my granny dress. "Nope, it's not about the treasure for us," I tell the knight. "We're going there to get—"

"A powerful magic item," Pan interrupts.

"Yeah, that's right!" Moxie chimes in. "For a wizard. And you'll never guess how we're going to find it! By digging through a big old stinking—"

"Dragon's lair," Pan finishes.

"Well, yeah," I giggle. "But once we're there, we're looking for a big doody!"

Pan's cheeks flush red. "He means we seek to do our *duty*."

"Um, sure. But don't forget the caca!" I remind her.

Pan jumps in, flustered. "He means don't forget how *gaga* we are to complete this quest."

She steps in front of me and turns to the knight. "You see, it's possible that this magic item we seek may have the power to heal the wizard's ailing mother," she explains. She shoots a quick look back at us. "Proper heroes. On a proper quest."

What's with this elf? The funniest part of this whole quest is that it involves a big steaming pile of poopy doo-doo. But Pan seems determined to leave out the punch line.

But the knight is impressed. Seraphim stands, wrapping her cloak around her against the chill. "Wow. That's really brave, you guys. Sincerely."

"Yeah," mumbles Sparkles from behind us. "And also not too smart. No offense. I mean, you guys could get seriously melted into a puddle. That would be *très* unattractive."

"Wait!" TickTock cries, jumping to his feet. "Tick-Tock is having a brilliant idea! Seraphim, Knight of the Rose . . . you should be coming with us!"

Sparkles whinnies in alarm. "Okay, that's, like, the complete opposite of a brilliant idea."

"Sparkles is right, TickTock," Pan interjects. "They clearly have more noble business to attend to."

I'm with Pan.

"TickTock, these two don't have time to hang out with us," I say. "They've got armor to shine. Shroomies to obliterate. And that cutie-poo prince isn't going to save himself."

But Moxie and TickTock aren't listening. "No way! It's perfect!" Moxie cries, jumping to her feet. "We could really use a brave knight on a quest like this!"

"And the noble steed!" TickTock adds, smiling broadly at the spoonicorn. "Don't be forgetting the noble steed!"

"I see what you're doing there, TickTock," says Sparkles. "You're buttering me up. And it's not working! Tell 'em, Sera!"

"Calm your hooves, Sparkles." The knight paces. She rubs her hand absently along the edge of her bow.

"The wizard's old mom lady is needing you, Seraphim," TickTock pleads.

"We need you, Seraphim!" says Moxie.

Seraphim gazes into the fire, lost in thought, eyes dancing green and gold with the reflection of the flames.

Finally she clears her throat and turns to us. "I think Sparkles and I could take a detour to a dragon's lair." A crooked smile splits her face. "To be honest, it sounds like a party."

Sparkles flops to the ground and covers her head with her hooves. "I don't see how that's a party," she mutters.

SUPERHEROIC ACHIEVEMENT!
Join Forces with a Noble Knight!
(300 Experience Points Awarded)

Moxie and TickTock cheer for the knight. Pan smiles

nervously. "That is very kind of you," she says to the knight. "But I don't think—"

"We insist," says Seraphim with a smile and a bow.

Pan lets out a breath and returns the bow. "Very well. Then afterward we will return the favor. We will help you retrieve the kidnapped prince."

"We will?" I ask.

"Fierce," says Seraphim.

"Fierce," says Moxie.

"Fierce," says TickTock.

"Okay, fine," says Sparkles. "But if you guys get me melted, I am never ever forgiving you. No offense."

The next morning, we move out early. Seraphim and Sparkles ride behind us. Rear guard, they call it. In case any shroomies try to sneak up on us from behind.

Which, I admit, I never would have thought of. Must be nice to be "a Knight of the Rose" and "good at everything" and "never cause banana explosions."

Seriously. Must be nice.

As we ride along, Moxie has questions. She turns to Pan.

"Hey, what was all that last night?" she asks the elf.

"All what?" Pan says innocently.

"You were acting so weird around Seraphim," says Moxie.

"Yeah," I add. "Every time I brought up the dragon dookie, you cut me off."

"Oh, that," she says nervously. "Sorry. I just..."

"Is it me?" I ask. I cross my arms self-consciously and try to hide my robes. "It's me, isn't it? You're embarrassed of my granny dress."

"What? No!" Pan hangs her head sheepishly. "I just... I don't know. Seraphim is so..."

"Cool?" asks Moxie.

"Super cool?" agrees TickTock.

"Perfect?" I say with a sniff. "Don't forget perfect."

Pan clears her throat. "I was going to say forthright. And regal. And honorable. And noble. But yes. Cool."

"She *is* pretty dang noble," says Moxie with a nod. "I mean, she probably slays dragons for breakfast and volunteers at a soup kitchen for lunch."

"Exactly," says Pan. "She reminds me of... my mother. A proper hero. On a proper quest." Pan grimaces. "I just couldn't bear telling her that we're going to the dragon's lair to..."

She hesitates.

"To scoop some poop," Moxie finishes for her.

"Yes," says Pan softly. "Stupid, isn't it?"

"No way," says Moxie with a reassuring smile. "I totally get it."

"Is that why you didn't want her to come with us?" I ask.

"Partly," says Pan. "But for another reason as well." Her eyebrows furrow together. "We are only on this quest because of me. It's bad enough that I'm putting you three in danger so that I can see my mother once again. But to put two complete strangers at risk . . . it does not feel right."

"Pffft," snorts Moxie. "I think Seraphim can handle herself."

"Yes," says Pan with a nod. "Agreed."

"And don't worry about us," says Moxie. "Together, there's nothing the four of us can't conquer. Right, Fart?"

"Yeah." I nod. "Sure."

Moxie turns back to Pan. "We'll bust into that dragon's lair. We'll do a little poo scuba when Seraphim's not looking. Bingo, bango, bongo, our noble quest is complete!"

"Yeah," says TickTock. "And then elf-girl gets to say hello to her mom lady!"

Pan shakes her head admiringly at us. "Thank you, my friends. I only hope it goes that smoothly. If anything bad happens to you because of me, I will never forgive myself."

And that's when something bad happens to us.

KER-BAMM!

One of our wheels hits a big boulder, sending Moxie tumbling backward into the dirt. The terrain got rocky when we weren't looking. No biggie for Bizzy. She just flies on, tugging us behind her.

KA-SLAMMO!

We bang into a huge rut.

WHACKA-BLAM!

We catapult forward as the cart lurches to a stop.

"Nice driving, Banana Boy," Sparkles says to me, trotting up.

I sigh. I'm really starting to dislike this spoonicorn.

"I'm not the one driving," I point out. "The bee is."

"Either way," says Seraphim, pointing. "Your wheel is shot."

She's right. Our fancy cart is now useless. Looks like we're hoofing it from here.

A chill wind blows, echoing eerily through the huge crags and steep cliffs. We stare up at the jagged hills that rise up before us. And beyond that . . . snow.

We've arrived at the Frostflung Mountains.

CHAPTER TEN

Making a fire is my number one job. With the help of my Cozy Camp spell, I can make a fire better than anybody.

But everything about this snow-shrouded land is cold and wet. Including the firewood. So our first night in the Frostflung Mountains is less than cozy.

We burrow deep into our coats and shiver. I snuggle under my robes and drift away, dreaming of a quest involving sipping a fruity drink on a sunny beach.

I think my dream is leaking into reality, because when I start to stir, the sun is shining. And I'm feeling super toasty.

But dang. No fruity drink.

Then I hear the crackle of wood burning. Impossible.

I peek out from under my robes. There's a nice blaze going. I can't believe it.

"I thought Fart said making a fire was impossible," says Pan.

Sparkles snorts, glancing over at my sleeping form. "Not for Seraphim."

Sure. Fine. Great. Who needs Cozy Camp when you've got Seraphim? Who needs a worthless mage when you've got a Knight of the Rose?

The knight pulls out a packet of sausages and starts to cook them over the fire. Normally that would be my cue to get up. Sausage is my built-in wake-up call. But I decide to stay put and soak up the remaining warmth of my robe fort. Just five more minutes.

"So tell me, ladies," Seraphim says. "What brings you on this quest?"

"We're after a powerful magic item," Moxie reminds her.

"But, like, how come?" asks Sparkles. "This wizard who needs to heal his mama. Did he promise you a big bag of gold?"

"Nope," Moxie blurts out. "He's going to bring Pan's dead mom back to life!"

Peeking through my covers, I see Moxie cringe,

suddenly horrified. "Pan! I'm so sorry!" she cries, turning to the elf. "That's personal! I shouldn't have . . ."

But Pan smiles. "No, it's okay, Moxie." She turns to Seraphim with a look of calm resolve. "The Great and Powerful Kevin promised that if we bring him this magic item, he'll let me say one last goodbye to my mother."

Seraphim reaches out and places a tender hand on Pan's shoulder. "Sheesh, I'm sorry, sis. What happened to your mom?"

This knight doesn't know Pan. But I do. Pan's not ready to talk about this. When she is, Moxie and I will be the first to know. She's not going to bare her soul to a couple of complete strangers.

Pan looks my way. She sees that TickTock and I are both asleep. And then she does it.

She bares her soul to a couple of complete strangers.

"My mother's name was *Cellaphallasanaes*," Pan says slowly. "Cypress Silversnow in your language."

Okay, then. Apparently she *is* ready to talk about it. Without me.

"My mother was a noble and powerful mage," Pan explains. "A teacher at Krakentop Academy. She died in a battle with a manticore on the island of Blackrook Reach."

"You were there?" asks the knight, poking the fire. "You saw it happen?"

"No," says Pan solemnly. "I was a young girl. This was about fifty years ago or so."

"Fifty years?" cries Sparkles. "How were you a young girl fifty years ago?"

Pan smiles. "Elves live for thousands of years. We age differently than humans."

"Oh, yeah. Sure, sure." Sparkles nods. "I knew that."

Pan keeps going. "Back then, many students that graduated from Krakentop Academy died within six months after leaving the school. Slain by orcs. Eaten by zombies. They were still too inexperienced. Too immature."

"What about Hero Wilderness Training?" asks Moxie.

"It didn't exist back then," answers Pan.

"What's Hero Wilderness Training?" asks Seraphim.

Moxie scooches closer to the fire and rubs her hands together for warmth. "It happens during the last year of school. Before graduation. You go with your master out into the wild and have real actual adventures. Fighting monsters. Slaying baddies. Real hero stuff for the first time ever. But with your master at your side."

Pan nods. "Before that, students simply studied,

graduated, and went out to face the world with no real-life experience."

"Yikes." Moxie cringes.

"Yikes is right," says Pan. "My mother saw how many students just weren't ready." Pan tucks some stray hair-wispies behind her pointed ears, lost in thought. "So she took a semester off from Krakentop and escorted a small group of new graduates on their first quest."

"Aw!" says Sparkles. "Like a mini wilderness trainy thing!"

Pan nods. "Exactly. And most of the students responded well to her charisma and solemn nature. But some were cocky. Now that they were Krakentop graduates, they thought they could face anything unscathed. One member of her group, a young mage, was particularly foolhardy."

"What happened?" asks Seraphim, hanging on Pan's words.

"They were on a quest to defeat a berserk manticore that was plaguing the countryside of Blackrook Reach." Pan stares into the distance, lost in the memories. "They had tracked the beast to its lair. But the young mage kept goofing off. Kept playing practical jokes on the others. As

MANTICORE

Beastly face.

Lion body.

Scorpion tail.

they crept outside the manticore's lair, my mother was kneeling, preparing her Lightning Fork spell. Just as she sat down to cast the spell, there was a loud . . ."

Pan hesitates.

"A loud what?" asks Moxie eagerly.

The elf glances my way, seems reluctant to continue. Then she speaks. "A loud . . . fart sound."

"Ew!" cries Sparkles. "Just ew!"

"The young mage had put a whoopee cushion under her. He thought he was being funny. The sound startled my mother. She miscast her spell. Her Lightning Fork fizzled, hitting some nearby rocks and rousing the manticore from its lair. Her spell would have finished the creature off there and then. Instead the beast put its stinger right through her heart."

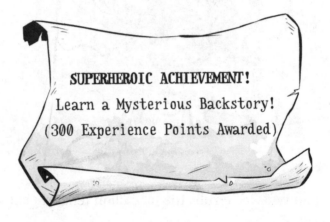

SUPERHEROIC ACHIEVEMENT!
Learn a Mysterious Backstory!
(300 Experience Points Awarded)

There's silence. The only sound is sausages sizzling.

"Everyone in the group died," whispers Pan finally. "Except the young mage."

"How did you find out about it?" asks Seraphim.

"The young mage came to our home in the elven kingdom of Kirajoy. Plagued with sorrow, he told my father the story and confessed to causing my mother's death. And he brought this."

"Your mom's necklace," says Moxie softly.

Pan nods. She rubs the medallion tenderly between her fingers.

"My father gave it to me. He said that my mother had placed a special enchantment within it. That it would draw me close to her, wherever I go."

Seraphim reaches out to palm the small medallion hanging from Pan's neck. "Simple design," she says, examining it carefully. "Classic. You would never guess that it's magical or enchanted."

"The necklace itself is not," replies Pan. "But buried at its core is a rare silversnow diamond. It is the diamond that carries the enchantment."

"And does it?" asks Seraphim, eyeing the necklace.

"Does it what?"

"Does it bring you closer to your mom?" the knight says.

Pan's eyes linger on the pendant, her fingers tracing the simple pattern. "I do not know," she finally says. "I suppose it helps me remember her." She wavers, her words coming slowly. "It's odd. There are times when I feel the sensation that . . . I don't know how to describe it . . . that if I were only to listen close enough, I could find her again. Which is ludicrous, of course."

"What did your dad do to that mage?" Sparkles asks, pawing the ground with an angry hoof. "Mr. Whoopee Cushion McButthead?"

Pan shrugs. "He let him go."

The spoonicorn snorts indignantly. "Jeez Louise. I would have horse-kicked him right in the nether regions."

Pan smirks in amusement. "I appreciate that." She stares at the mist-shrouded peaks. "I always regretted that I never got to say goodbye to her. I have always wondered . . . what if that young mage hadn't been in her group?" Her voice putters out. "Perhaps my mother would still be alive."

A hush settles over our camp as everyone absorbs this. Pan shakes the thoughts away and tucks the necklace under her tunic.

"And this Kevin character," Seraphim says. "He's going to conjure up your mom for you if you get him this magic item?"

"That's what he says," replies Moxie.

Seraphim pulls the sausages from the fire. "Then we better make sure you succeed," she says. She eyes Pan thoughtfully. "Who was it?" she asks. "The young mage?"

Pan shrugs. "My father never told me the boy's name. Nobody of consequence. I'm sure his foolish nature led to his death long ago."

The four of them eat in silence. But in my fort of robes, my heart aches. For Pan, of course.

But also . . . if I'm really honest . . .

Because Pan shared this story with Seraphim. And not me.

"Well, enough of that!" Pan rises. She grabs her bo staff and twirls it deftly. "I need to center myself before we continue our journey."

"You should work out," suggests Moxie. "Do a little sparring! That always makes you feel better."

That's my cue. Pan and I spar together almost every afternoon. It's a little early for my taste, but I start to stir. After all, this is our special thing. And my friend needs me.

"Good idea." Pan turns to the knight. "Seraphim, would you spar with me?"

The knight rises and bows. "Sis, it would be my honor."

A cold chill settles over me that has nothing to do with the temperature. Apparently my friend *doesn't* need me. She has Seraphim.

I feel a hoof in my stomach.

"Up and at 'em, sleepmaster general," says the spoonicorn. "We need more firewood."

Stupid spoonicorn.

Maybe at the next town we can replace her with something less annoying. Like a nice quiet horse. Or a swarm of mosquitos. Or a pack of bloodthirsty hyenas. Anything, really.

But I guess she's part of the package. We got stuck with her when we were joined by Seraphim.

Seraphim.

How did we manage for so long without her? I wonder bitterly. I mean, she can do anything.

She can battle shroomies without conjuring up an explosive fruit salad.

She can make a fire, no magic required.

She's a good listener.

She can even spar with Pan.

All the things I used to do. Only she does them better.

I'm starting to think . . . maybe Sparkles isn't the one getting replaced.

CHAPTER ELEVEN

The higher we go, the louder the wind howls. It's like some beast in the distance, waiting to be fed. Bizzy huddles close to me, fluttering low against the wind.

We've been trudging through a snowstorm for three days.

Trudge, trudge, trudge.

Trudging for three days gives you time to reflect on your choices. Examine life's little lessons.

And I've learned a few things.

Thing One: These shoes were not made for trudging. Nor were these legs. Nor was this whole body. I miss my comfy cushion in my bee-drawn cart.

Thing Two: Thank goodness Pan thinks of everything.

Like these coats. Right now my fingers are frozen. My toes are ice cubes. My hat is a snow cone. If it weren't for this coat, I'd be a mage-flavored Popsicle for sure.

And Thing Three: I can officially confirm . . . spoonicorns are super annoying. At least this one is. If I hear the words "Banana Boy" one more time, I may lose it.

"Don't you *do* anything?" I ask Sparkles as we trudge. "I mean besides hand out vaguely insulting nicknames?"

"What do you mean, *do* anything?" she responds. "I do all kinds of things! Offer helpful fashion advice. Give incredible makeovers. Boost morale with my upbeat attitude and natural good looks."

"I mean powers," I say. "Aren't unicorns—"

She shoots me a dirty look.

"Sorry," I say. "Aren't *spoonicorns* supposed to have powers?"

"I have loads of powers," she says. "The power of persuasion, for one. I'm super charming."

"That's not a power," I point out.

"Let me finish!" the spoonicorn squawks. "I'm also an a-MAZ-ing singer. Singer-songwriter, actually. I have a voice that will literally rock you to your core. I need to baby it right now because of the chill. But maybe one day I'll give a little concert."

"She *is* a good singer," confirms Seraphim.

"Plus I can dance *and* act," Sparkles goes on. "I'm a triple threat. The total package."

"Those aren't really powers," I point out. "I mean *magic* powers."

"Oh, yeah!" cries Moxie. "Like, can you fly?"

"Moxie. Sweetie," says Sparkles. "You're thinking of a pegasus."

"Can you heal people?" asks Pan. "With your magical horn? I mean your magical spoon?"

"Oh my gosh, you guys," she says. "That's a unicorn thing. Plus sick people are kind of gross. Am I right?"

"Then what?" asks TickTock. "What is being so magical about this spoon?"

"Here! Hold out your hand." Sparkles lowers her head, touching her spoon to TickTock's open palm. There's a blinding sparkle of light from the tip. When it fades away, something is left behind in TickTock's hand. Something on a stick. Something rainbow-colored. Something . . . kitty-shaped.

"Whoa!" says Moxie in awe. "Do me! Do me!"

One by one, the spoonicorn

creates whimsical sherbet pops for Moxie, Pan, and Seraphim. A smiley face. A heart. And a bunny.

"Sherbet pops?" I ask incredulously. *"That's* your impressive magic power?"

"Hey now," the spoonicorn says. "I don't see *you* conjuring up fruity delicious treats with the magical spoon growing out of *your* forehead."

Pan licks the stick. "It's delicious," she says.

"Well, shoot," I say sheepishly. "Now I want one."

"Mm-hmm. Now who's got impressive magic powers?" But she waltzes over, bends down, and zaps my hand with her spoon.

I'm holding a sherbet pop. In the shape of a little pile of poop. A poop pop.

Sparkles gives me a sassy smile. "Taste the rainbow, Banana Boy."

After four days of trudging, the sun finally comes out. Everybody's more upbeat. We're even joking around and throwing snowballs. And then we see it.

The ravine.

A bottomless chasm yawns before us. Okay, probably not bottomless. There's gotta be a bottom down there somewhere. Covered with pools of acid. And monsters. And spikes.

It's at least two hundred feet to the other side. And dangling across the expansive gap, swaying precariously in the wind . . . is a rope bridge.

"Who built a rope bridge way up here?" asks Moxie, eyeing the frayed ropes.

"Is not a bridge," cries TickTock over the howl of the wind. "Look closer!"

He's right. Ropes run from one side to the other. But there are no planks. There are no steps. Suspended from the ropes by a series of gears and levers . . . is a little cart. A rope boat. A sky ride.

"It is being a gondola!" cries TickTock.

Sure. That was my next guess. A gondola.

"Fine," says Moxie. "Who built a super-cool but incredibly rickety gondola way up here?"

Pan yanks a wicked-looking arrow from one of the hideously carved posts. "Goblins. That's who."

"Probably the froblins that Kevin warned us about," I suggest.

TickTock steps up and turns a crank. The little cable car starts moving. Gears whir and pistons pump, bringing the gondola smoothly to our side of the chasm. "Piston-pump action!" he cries. "With rotating spanner sprockets!"

"I literally love the way you talk, TickTock," says Sparkles enthusiastically. "It is *très* technical. Am I right? It's like you're saying so much while simultaneously communicating almost nothing. I just adore it."

The gondola glides fluidly to a stop in front of us.

"Is very strange," says TickTock. "Very clever and intricate design."

"Why is that so strange?" asks Pan.

"Being way too clever for goblins to build," replies TickTock. "Is making TickTock nervous."

Bizzy whimpers at my side.

"I'm with the bee," says Sparkles apprehensively. "This bridge thingy is giving me the serious heebies."

"Calm your hooves, Sparkles," warns Seraphim, drawing her bow. We eye the craggy peaks, searching for some sign of an ambush.

But there's nothing. Only a blanket of white. And the wind howling at us.

"I don't think we have a choice," I say.

The only way we're getting to the top of the mountain is across this chasm.

The gondola wobbles precariously as Moxie steps onto it. But she leads us aboard anyway. We pile in slowly, Seraphim and Sparkles bringing up the rear.

I have no idea how to work this crazy contraption, but TickTock is in his element. He grabs a handle and starts cranking. And ever so slowly, we begin to glide across the gap.

SUPERHEROIC ACHIEVEMENT!
Ride a Neato Gondola!
(300 Experience Points Awarded)

We're about halfway across when the wind picks up.

"That's odd," says Pan.

"What's odd?" I ask, trying not to look down at the drop below us.

"The howling of the wind has gotten louder, but the gondola isn't swaying any harder," she says.

"Who cares about the wind?!" cries Moxie, pointing at the other side of the chasm. "Look!"

There, crowding the far side of the gorge. Froblins. Lots and lots of froblins.

Fur-trimmed masks cover their faces, protecting them from the cold. But there's no mistaking their raggedy goblin armor. And their jaggedy goblin spears. And their gaggedy goblin smell.

"Go back!" shouts Moxie. "We can't fight them in this thing! About-face!"

TickTock throws the thing in reverse, and we start to go the other way. But almost immediately the phibling slams us to a stop.

"What's the holdup?!" I cry.

"That is being a holdup!" yells TickTock, pointing back the way we came.

I rub my eyes and hope I'm dreaming.

Because back where we started . . . is the source of the howling. And it's not the wind.

"Crud on a cracker," I cry.

It's a yeti.

ROOOOOAR!

CHAPTER TWELVE

We are trapped in a goblin-yeti sandwich.

Seraphim draws her bow and sends a rain of arrows at the yeti. But they bounce off its tough furry pelt and into the ravine below.

My turn. I've got a nice little spell up my sleeve called Puppy Power. It'll transform this bloodthirsty beastie into a baby beagle before you can say "woof."

I hunker behind Bizzy. Make the gestures. Say the incantation. *"Pepper-puppy-papyrus!"* My spell sparkles through the air, hits the beast, and fizzles into nothingness.

"It's magic resistant!" Moxie cries. She has one hand on the gondola and the other on Buzzlock's book. "None of your magic mumbo jumbo is gonna get through that thick skin!"

YETI

Three thousand pounds of frozen ugly.

Can smell fresh meat from miles away.
Smarter than it looks.
Thick magic-resistant hide.

"It's probably not smart enough to use the mechanism and haul us back to it," says Pan.

As if hearing her words, the yeti lets out a screaming roar. It reaches for the rope. And like some oversize angry gorilla, it begins to climb, hand over hand, out to us.

And still the yeti keeps coming.

Its muscles bulge. Its horns glint in the frosty sunlight. Its fanged mouth froths with spit.

The dinner bell has rung. And the yeti is hungry.

Seraphim bristles. "I'm not gonna just sit here and wait to get plucked from the air by this jumbo snow-squatch." She pulls a vicious-looking dagger from her belt. "Hold on, everybody!"

That's all the warning we get. Then Seraphim cuts the rope.

You know, that rope that was holding our gondola perilously over the gorge?

You know, that rope that was our only lifeline between soaring through the air and dropping like a stone?

That's the rope.

I feel the gondola give way under my feet, and I scramble to grab the railing.

My stomach plummets as we drop . . . drop . . . drop . . . and then . . .

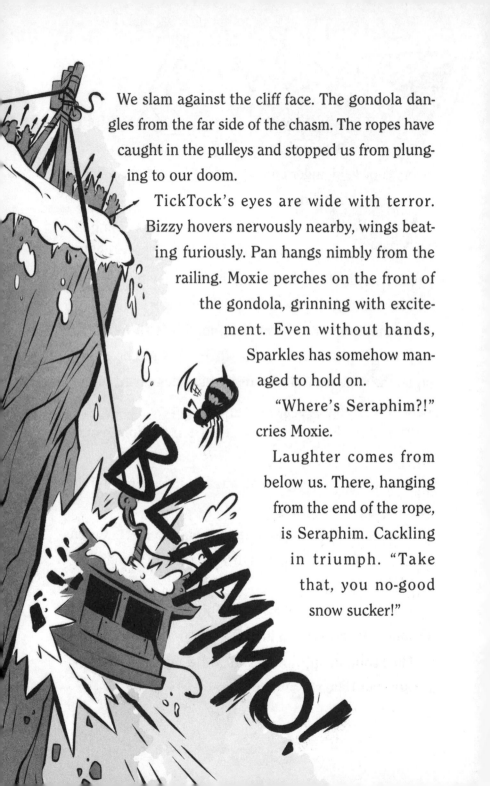

We slam against the cliff face. The gondola dangles from the far side of the chasm. The ropes have caught in the pulleys and stopped us from plunging to our doom.

TickTock's eyes are wide with terror. Bizzy hovers nervously nearby, wings beating furiously. Pan hangs nimbly from the railing. Moxie perches on the front of the gondola, grinning with excitement. Even without hands, Sparkles has somehow managed to hold on.

"Where's Seraphim?!" cries Moxie.

Laughter comes from below us. There, hanging from the end of the rope, is Seraphim. Cackling in triumph. "Take that, you no-good snow sucker!"

BLAMMO!

Our eyes dart to the other side of the ravine. Clinging to the cliff face is the yeti. It's managed to catch itself, but jagged rocks have slashed painful gouges across its face. It howls in anger and scrambles up the bluff, back to the top of the cliff.

Seeing that we're out of reach, it gives one last roar of frustration. Angry froth spews from its throat. It hammers the ground with its fists. Then it turns, bounds over the snowy dunes, and disappears from sight.

"We're saved!" cries Moxie. "Yay for Seraphim!"

SUPERHEROIC ACHIEVEMENT!
Thwart a Yeti Attack!
(300 Experience Points Awarded)

WHIZZSH!

A spear whizzes past us from the cliff face above. From the froblins.

Oh, yeah. Them.

Another flies past, barely missing Bizzy.

"I take it back!" yells Moxie. "We're not saved!"

We are helpless. Dangling like worms on a hook. There's no way to fight. There's nowhere to run.

There's only one thing left to do. Use our words.

I cast Magic Mouth.

"Stop!" I cry. "We surrender! We don't want to fight!"

But it comes out all *Snaazzxkl wix zaxxxleglakkzz!* with way too many *z*'s and *x*'s. Yep. I'm speaking in Goblin.

"What are you doing?" cries Seraphim.

"Talking to them," I reply.

"Oh my gosh! That is such a good idea," says Sparkles. "They're probably, like, totally the talking type."

Okay, I can't tell if she's being serious or sarcastic. She's got this unsettling gift for being super encouraging while completely insulting you at the same time. I think that's actually her true spoonicorn power.

To be fair, these are frost goblins, after all, not a nice reasonable water weirdo. But I have to try something.

At least the spears have stopped raining down.

Then from up above comes an answer. Not in Goblin.

Through the magic of my spell, I know instinctively what language is being spoken to me.

In a flash, I remember a lesson from Master Elmore.
An overview of humanoid races.

Now see here, Fart. There are important cultural differences between the races to be aware of.

Aren't people pretty much just people?

No! An elf is not a gnome and a dwarf is not a goblin!

Elves value nature. Gnomes value mechanics. Dwarves value gold and loyalty.

And goblins . . . well, goblins do not value anything at all!

But in this moment, I value that lesson from my former master. Because I suddenly know what to do.

"TickTock!" I cry. "Your little metal guy!"

He looks up at me with wide orange eyes. "TickTock's mech-man?"

"Sure!" I nod. "Whatever! Give it to me!"

The phibling digs into his backpack and draws out his shiny creation. "Is not a boom-bot!" TickTock hollers.

I don't know what that means. And there's no time for chitchat. I snatch the doohickey and speak the words to another spell. Gas Attack. *"Flatulencia."*

POOF!

The spell turns me into a smelly gas cloud. Not just me. Me, my clothes, and anything I'm holding. I float away, metal man and all.

"Banana Boy!" Sparkles calls after me. "Don't leave us! Right when I was starting to really like you!"

It's weird being gaseous. I mean, I've been gaseous loads of times. Don't even get near me after I eat brussels sprouts. But actually *being* gaseous . . . well, it's a strange sensation.

I float to the top of the cliff and hover in front of the swarm of froblins. They eyeball my cloud nervously.

FLUMP! I rematerialize before them. Spears raise,

ready to stab me through the heart and end my magic-making days.

But I hold out the . . . what did TickTock call it? The mech-man.

The froblins lower their spears.

One in the front, the leader, reaches up and removes his fur-shrouded mask.

The eyes behind the mask aren't glittering with cruelty and hate. Instead eager eyes stare at the mechanical wonder held before him.

Because these aren't frost goblins. Goblins value nothing. But gnomes value mechanics.

And these are gnomes.

CHAPTER THIRTEEN

With the gift of the mech-man, the mood on the cliff takes a dramatic shift. Spears are replaced with smiles.

In two minutes flat, the gnomes have hauled my friends up to safety, gondola and all.

They surround us and lead us away in a gaggle of chatter. Guiding us along some path that only they can see, they take us farther into the mountains, past frost-covered peaks and deep drifts of snow.

"Where are they taking us?" asks Moxie.

I ask the lead gnome. He responds in his growly language. Even with the magic of my spell, I'm not sure I fully understand.

"He says 'meanwhile,'" I tell my friends. "I'm not sure what that means."

"Well, I guess we'll find out soon enough," says Pan.

And we do. Because thirty minutes later we round an icy bend. And something shocking comes into view.

The remains of . . . a ship. Or part of a ship. I have no idea how it got way up here in the mountains. But the gnomes have turned the hull into an elaborate entrance that leads into a deep cave.

They shed their stinking goblin clothes and crude weapons, hanging them on hooks. Then they lead us inside.

We've been in caves. Horrible kraken lairs, gross with slime and bones. The Caves of Catastrophe, filled with oozy things and the stink of ogres. This isn't like those.

The hall the gnomes lead us down is brightly lit and spotlessly clean. Warmth emanates from below, and echoes hint at a larger chamber. Turning a corner, we gasp in awe.

It's an underground town of hissing steam and whirring contraptions. A mechanical wonderland. But also somehow sad. Rusty. Run-down. Like it was all made from leftover parts and salvaged scrap.

"This-a Meanwhile," says our guide in Gnomish.

I don't know what that means. And I don't care. It's amazing.

TickTock gazes around him adoringly, humming along to the sounds of clicking and clacking like it's music to his amphibious ears.

The lead gnome, still clutching our little mech-man in his grimy fist, waves us down a steam-shrouded path. We finally stop at a massive mechanical door.

The lead gnome speaks to the guard there in their guttural language.

"Where-a big Boss-King Grease-Ratchet?"

"Him inside. Take-a bath."

"Again? Always in bath. Or in battledome."

"What you want me to say-a? Him like-a bath! Him like-a battledome!"

"Gotta these tall-ones. Seeya boss-king quick-fast."

"Him in bath!"

"I know him in bath! But seeya anyway! Bring-a this!"

He holds out TickTock's mech-man.

The guard's eyes go wide. He turns a dial on the door, triggering a series of ropes, gears, and pulleys. The door swings open, and our escort leads us through.

"What's going on, Fart?" asks Moxie, nervously gripping her hammer. "You can still understand them, right?"

"Yeah. They're taking us to see their king," I tell my friends. "Somebody named Grease-Ratchet."

"Grease-Ratchet?" Sparkles asks, tilting her head to the side. "Are you sure you're translating that right? That doesn't sound like a very king-y name. King Fairyblossom Dottingham the Third. King Tuxedo Mc-Sequins. *Those* are literally the king-iest names ever. Am I right?"

"More importantly," says Pan, "are we prisoners of this Grease-Ratchet? Or guests?"

"I'm not sure yet," I tell them. Bizzy flutters close, but I pat her reassuringly. "I think we're about to find out."

Hot air comes billowing out as we enter the chamber. The walls glow red from a natural lava spring. Giant wheels are being turned by gnomes, fueling gizmos that churn the lava and funnel it under a huge tub. In the tub, submerged in steaming brown sludge, is a stout gnome.

"Boss-King!" grunts our escort. "Boss-King!"

Grease-Ratchet sits up, annoyed.

"Whatta for you barge-in boss-king bath?"

"Gotta tall-ones. Find at pit-gorge cross-place. Cutta down gondola."

"He's telling him that we cut down their gondola," I translate.

"Oh no," says Sparkles. "That's *très* bad, am I right?"

"Cutta down gondola! Why you not cutta them down speedy-quick? Why you bring-a to Boss-King?"

"Them clever! Getta way from yeti."

"Not clever! Tall! Dumb! Take-a way. Letta Grease-Ratchet enjoy grease-bath!"

"Yes, clever! Them give-a me this!"

He holds aloft TickTock's creation. And the boss-king's jaw drops. He's no longer interested in the joys of his grease bath. He only has eyes for the mechanical man.

Grease-Ratchet grabs the mech-man.

"Mmm-hmm. Mmm-hmm. You right! Tall-ones maybe clever!"

"He thinks we're clever," I translate. "Because of TickTock's little gizmo-guy."

"Well done, TickTock," whispers Pan. "They obviously

value all things mechanical. Your ingenuity may have saved us once again."

"Oh, yay!" says Moxie hopefully. "That's *très* good, am I right?"

"What you want-a me to do with tall-ones, Boss-King?"

One of the nearby gnomes hands the boss-king a towel. He drapes it around himself and steps, dripping, from his grease bath.

"What you think-a? Boss-King Grease-Ratchet wanna see how clever tall-ones be."

He smiles widely as he looks down at us.

"Put-a tall-ones in battledome."

He snaps his fingers. Dozens of gnomes appear instantly, pointing spears at us. Moxie instinctively starts to raise her hammer. But she hesitates. We are badly outnumbered. And surrounded.

"I guess this means we're prisoners?" says Pan.

"Not exactly." I gulp. "He wants to put us in the battledome."

"Did you say *battledome*?" squeaks Sparkles. "That's, like, the definition of *très bad*. If you look up *très bad* in the dictionary, it literally says *see battledome*."

"Everybody relax," says Moxie with a grin. "Sounds like we'll at least have a fighting chance. And I'll take a good fight any day." She turns to the knight. "Am I right, Seraphim?"

There's no answer.

"Seraphim?"

We turn to look.

But there's no Seraphim.

The knight is gone.

CHAPTER FOURTEEN

None of us know when we last saw Seraphim. She was with us at the gondola. Moxie swears she talked to her as we traveled to the gnome cave. But nobody saw her slip away.

"We should be pleased," says Pan. "Perhaps she escaped."

But we don't have time to celebrate Seraphim's sneaky escape. That's 'cuz we're being dragged off by a chattering pack of gnomes to fight for our lives in some battledome of doom.

The gnomes keep a cautious eye on Bizzy's stinger, but they haven't taken our weapons. Maybe they don't consider us a threat. Of course, we're a thousand feet underground surrounded by hundreds of gnomes. Maybe that's why. Maybe.

We enter a large metal building, and the guards drag us into some sort of holding chamber. On the far side, a gated door leads into a circular arena. Tiers of seats surround the arena, already filling with spectators.

The battledome.

"That's not very much room to fight," Moxie says, peeking through the bars. She looks at Pan and me.

The guard hands TickTock's little mech-man back to me. He chatters away and points to the arena behind the gate.

But I can no longer understand him.

Magic is a weird and wacky thing. Spells don't last forever. They wear off. Expire. Like cheese.

I can cast a spell again once it wears off. In theory. But magic takes a ton of energy, and some spells drain me more than others. It's like there's a juice box of magical energy inside me. There's only so much hocus-pocus in the juice box.

And between days of trudging and all the magic-making I did during the yeti attack, I can tell . . . the juice box is dry.

The gnome stares, waiting for a response.

"I'm sorry," I tell him, passing the mech-man to Tick-Tock. "My magic has worn off. I can't understand you."

The guard tilts his head in confusion.

"HE CAN'T UNDERSTAND YOU!" yells Sparkles. She whispers to me, "It's like we're speaking a totally different language. Am I right?"

He shakes his head in frustration. But then a thought seems to pop into his head. He snaps his fingers and grunts. One of the other guards dashes out.

"What's going on?" asks Pan.

"Not quite sure," I say.

The guard comes back in, dragging the tiniest little

gnome I've ever seen. Her glasses are huge, bigger than her head. They push her at us, and she stares up with curious eyes.

"Aw!" cries Sparkles. "Look at this little cutie standing there looking all cute!" She bends down to the tiny gnome and starts shouting. "HELLO THERE, WEIRD LITTLE CHICK! DO YOU SPEAK THE COMMON TONGUE?"

The little gnome clears her throat. "I speak-a the tall-talk good-quick," she says. "My name issa *Sprinzilesef*. You call-a me Knock-Knock."

KNOCK-KNOCK

Tiny.

Glasses.

Cute as a button.

Clever hands for making things.

"I know we're, like, literally on the verge of death and all, but I adore her," says Sparkles in amazement. "It's like, knock knock. Who's there? The most darling little gnome in the universe, that's who!"

The deafening roar of the battledome makes my teeth rattle in my mouth. Bizzy whimpers at my side. Boss-King Grease-Ratchet emerges at the center of the small stadium, quieting the crowd. He begins to address them in his growly language. They titter excitedly.

"What's going on?" asks Moxie, gripping and ungripping her hammer anxiously.

Knock-Knock listens intently. "Boss-King Grease-Ratchet announce-a you to the crowd right-quick," she says after a moment. "You getta ready to do battle. Battle to the death!"

The iron gate before us slowly begins to raise, opening the way between us and the arena. Grease-Ratchet hops out of the dome and seats himself in the front row, directly across from us.

The crowd goes nuts as soon as they see us.

"We understand that we have to fight," Pan says patiently, gripping her bo staff. "But *what*, Knock-Knock? *What* do we have to fight?"

"Tall-ones not fight!" cries Knock-Knock. "HIM fight!" She points to TickTock.

"The phibling?" asks Pan nervously. "TickTock has to fight all by himself?"

"No way!" roars Moxie. "Not cool!"

"HIM!" says Knock-Knock, pointing again. "HIM fight."

The guards seem to decide the time for talking has ended. They shove us through the gate, into the arena.

There's a roar from the crowd.

Boss-King Grease-Ratchet lowers something into the ring. Something metal. Something that gleams in the torchlight. Whatever it is, it starts to whirl and spin. Huge battle-axes emerge from the hard metal shell. They start smashing together, sending sparks over the delighted crowd.

Oh. My. Gosh. Grease-Ratchet has a mech-man of his own.

"Boss-King's bot named Chop-Chop," says Knock-Knock, staring nervously into the arena. She turns and points once again at TickTock. "HIM fight Chop-Chop! Fight Chop-Chop now!"

But she's not pointing at TickTock. The phibling's eyes follow the little gnome's finger . . . down to the mechanical man in his hands.

"Battledome issa not tall-one fight," Knock-Knock repeats. "Battledome issa bot fight!"

CHAPTER FIFTEEN

The roar of the crowd is deafening.

The guards lower the iron gate behind us. We're trapped in the arena with nothing between us and a battle-axe-wielding mech-man named Chop-Chop.

"You guys!" says Sparkles. "Are we going to die right now? Because I'm too beautiful to die!"

"Same here," says Moxie.

"Calm hooves!" TickTock cries at them. "Did friends not hear Knock-Knock? This is bot battle! Friends not have to fight Chop-Chop." He holds his mech-man out. "*Bronzebelly* have to fight Chop-Chop!"

Bronzebelly is half the size of Chop-Chop. Plus Chop-Chop's axes are no joke. They're big. They're sharp. And they're . . . axes.

BOT FIGHT!

BRONZEBELLY VS. CHOP-CHOP

"But what happens if our bot loses?" screeches Sparkles. "DO WE DIE? BECAUSE I'M TOO BEAUTIFUL TO DIE!"

I ignore her and grab the phibling by the shoulders. "TickTock, can't you just point Bronzebelly at their guy and make it blow up?" I ask. "Like you did with the tuskins that one time?"

"Tried to tell you at cliff," says TickTock. "Not the same model. That wind-up dragon was being TickTock's special boom-bot. Bronzebelly is not being a boom-bot."

"That's unfortunate," says Pan. "What does Bronzebelly do?"

TickTock cracks open a panel in the back of the gizmo. Peeking from the guts of the machinery are several small buttons and levers. The phibling pecks at them in order, obviously following some kind of predetermined sequence that only he knows. He closes the panel and sets the small mech-man down.

"Better stuffs," he says. A diabolical grin spreads across his froggy face. He throws a tiny switch, and the mech-man charges straight at Chop-Chop.

Little Bronzebelly barely rolls into range before the bigger bot starts hacking. But Bronzebelly has wheels, and Chop-Chop has legs, so it manages to dodge Chop-Chop's first few axe swings. But it doesn't take long for Chop-Chop to close the distance and do some serious damage.

WHA-CHOP!

One of Bronzebelly's arms falls to the floor under the mighty swing of Chop-Chop's battle-axe.

The crowd explodes with approval. Three hundred gnomes cry out as one: "*GVIGVILI!!!*"

I turn anxiously to Knock-Knock. "What are they saying?"

She thinks for a minute. "*Gvigvili.* It is like, how you say in the tall-talk, *yippee!* Or *hurray!* Or *I am so happy I could kiss a yeti on the mouth!* Like that."

I'm sorry I asked.

"Doesn't that thing have any weapons?" cries Moxie anxiously. "He's getting murdalized in there!"

"Just be waiting, Hammer-girl," says TickTock calmly. "Watching close."

Our eyes turn back to the battle. And just in time.

Bronzebelly's remaining arm unfolds and some sort of saw blade comes whirring out. The mech-man wheels in close to Chop-Chop, nimbly ducking an axe, and digs the whirring blade into the other bot's arm.

The arm, axe and all, clatters to the ground with a clang.

Grease-Ratchet's beefy face goes red. He leans in hungrily, as if willing his bot to exact vengeance.

And that's exactly what it does.

From the middle of Chop-Chop's chest a compartment opens up, revealing a small nozzle.

A stream of white-hot flame shoots out, enveloping poor little Bronzebelly.

TickTock's mech-man tries to wheel away, but there's no escaping the fiery blast. Bronzebelly's remaining arm melts away, sending the buzz saw clattering to the ground in a molten mess of gears, springs, and tubes.

But Grease-Ratchet and Chop-Chop are not satisfied with simply maiming TickTock's poor bot. Chop-Chop shoots a stream of flaming death straight at the smaller bot's face. The flame intensifies, melting Bronzebelly's head into a fiery puddle on the floor.

The mob roars in approval.

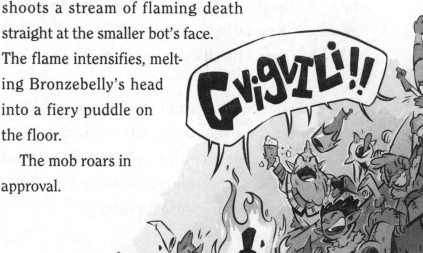

"Oh no," Pan whispers, horrified.

The phibling gulps back emotion. "It is being all right, elf-girl. Is only being weeks of work down the toilet. Is what Bronzebelly is made for."

"Still, TickTock," says Moxie, reaching for the phibling. "That guy totally melted your mech-man's face. I'm so sorry."

"It's so sad," says Sparkles. "Know what's even sadder? What they're going to do to our faces now that we lost the battledome."

"Oh, didn't lose the battledome, shiny pony," says TickTock casually. "Bronzebelly head is only being decorative."

Decorative? Our eyes shoot back to the bots.

Boss-King Grease-Ratchet stands on the railing, waving triumphantly at his people. Chop-Chop parades around the ring, taking a victory lap.

Nobody sees a hatch open up where Bronzebelly's head used to be. Except us.

Nobody notices the cauldron of liquid metal that emerges from the depths of the little bot. Except us.

Nobody is paying attention as Bronzebelly wheels silently up behind Chop-Chop and dumps a bucket of molten bronze over its opponent's head.

Except us.

The liquified metal begins to harden, encasing the gnome-made mech-man in a tomb of solid bronze.

"That's why TickTock is calling him Bronzebelly," says the phibling with a grin. "Got a bucket of melty-hot bronze in his belly."

What's left of Chop-Chop teeters to the ground with an echoing thud.

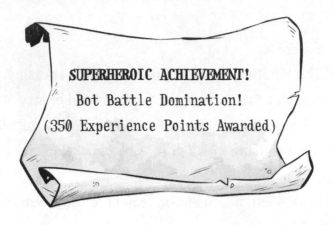

Silence hangs in the room. Horror is frozen on every gnome's face. All eyes turn to their shock-stricken boss-king.

Grease-Ratchet stands to his feet.

He glares at us.

And then he says it. The one word that seals our fate once and for all.

"GVIGVILI!!!"

At the look of joy and exultation on their leader's face, the crowd goes wild.

"GVIGVILI!!!"

Boss-King Grease-Ratchet stares hard at us. And he shoots us a big fat thumbs-up.

We crush TickTock in a hug and scream one word at the top of our lungs:

CHAPTER SIXTEEN

We are not prisoners. We are honored guests.

The cheers we receive at the celebration feast are proof of that.

Leg of winter wolf.

"Boss-King Grease-Ratchet say-a your bot fight real good-quick," says little Knock-Knock, translating for us. "He happy you come to us."

"Please give him our thanks," says Pan.

"Yeah, you tell him he didn't do too bad himself," says Seraphim. "That fire-torch thing was fierce."

SERAPHIM?!

There she sits, munching away on her winter-wolf dumplings like it's just another Tuesday.

"Seraphim!" hisses Moxie under her breath. "What happened to you?"

Baked snowtatoes.

Hard-boiled frost-wyrm egg.

"Oh! My! Gosh!" gasps Sparkles. "I haven't been so freaked out since my spoon got caught in that revolving door in Grayraven City. That's how you made me feel! Like I was stuck in a revolving door!"

Seraphim pats Sparkles comfortingly. "Sorry about that. When they first brought us in, I couldn't tell if we were guests or prisoners."

"So you snuck away," says Pan.

"Exactly," she says.

"Seraphim did sneaking!" says TickTock. "Following! Making escape plans!"

The knight grins. "The phibling gets it. I made myself scarce and followed you guys. In case things turned ugly and a rescue was required."

She fist-bumps the phibling. "Nice bot fighting, by the way. I haven't seen a match that good since the underground bot leagues in Dwarvenforge."

"You were in the crowd!" says Moxie. "Hidden!"

"Bull's-eye," says Seraphim smoothly. "You got me, sis."

Pan shakes her head in admiration. "It was a clever strategy," she says. "You are sneaky as well as noble."

"Two traits I admire the heck out of!" says Moxie, stuffing her mouth with pasta.

"Yeah," says Sparkles. "Literally, like, sneaky but noble too! Also if you ever leave me behind again, I will totally cut you, okay? No offense."

"Sparkles," the knight says, flashing that crooked smile of hers. "Would I ever leave you behind?"

The gnomes do not seem to notice the sudden re-appearance of Seraphim. I guess all us tall-ones look the same to them.

"Knock-Knock," Pan says to the little gnome. "When we first encountered your people at the gondola crossing, they were disguised as froblins."

"Yeah," I chime in. "Where are all the real froblins? These mountains are supposed to be crawling with them."

"No more," she says. "No more issa the frost goblins."

She shares a quick exchange with Grease-Ratchet, then turns back to us. "Boss-King say-a we not tell outsiders our story. But you not outsiders no more. Him say-a to tell you how us snomes come to be here."

"Snomes?" says Sparkles. "I thought it was pronounced like 'gnomes.' Is the *s* all silent?"

"Notta just gnomes," says Knock-Knock, wagging a tiny finger sternly. "Be-a *snow* gnomes. We call-a *snomes* in tall-talk. You getta comfy. I tell you all about it."

And so she does.

139

Pan sighs deeply, taking it all in. She turns to us. "That explains a lot. So this place we're heading is an old snome fortress called Tinkertop."

Knock-Knock overhears. "Tall-ones go to Tinkertop? Kill-a Glacierbane?"

"No, we're not going there to kill the dragon," I explain. "We're going there to get something."

Knock-Knock confers with her boss. Grease-Ratchet's eyes go wide. He chatters eagerly with the little snome, as if some new idea has hit him. An idea that Knock-Knock does not like one little bit.

Knock-Knock argues. Grease-Ratchet argues back.

Knock-Knock pleads. Grease-Ratchet sternly points back at us.

Knock-Knock sighs. "Boss-King say since you go to Tinkertop, you do little favor for Grease-Ratchet. While you be-a there."

I can guess what this "little favor" is. And the answer is NO. No way. No how. "We are NOT slaying the dragon for him," I say firmly.

"Not slay-a dragon," clarifies Knock-Knock. "You get something for Grease-Ratchet. Relic."

We look at one another, all thinking the same thought. Hordewrath.

"I'm afraid we cannot touch the dragon treasure," says Pan firmly. "Not a single gold piece."

"Not dragon treasure," says Knock-Knock. "Dragon treasure in main fortress. Grease-Ratchet's relic in Great Workshop. Around back. Dragon not care about workshop."

"What is it?" I ask nervously. "The relic."

"Special battle-bot," says the tiny snome. "Belong to boss-king's granddaddy. Very important to boss-king."

Pan turns to TickTock. "You know your way around mechanical things, TickTock. You could probably find this relic."

TickTock nods. "Yes. But TickTock is thinking snomes are maybe having many battle-bots in workshop. How will TickTock be knowing which one to take?"

Knock-Knock turns to Grease-Ratchet, pleading with the boss-king. But he won't listen to her. He shakes his head and points at us firmly. The little snome sighs in defeat.

"You will know," she says. "Because Knock-Knock issa going with you."

CHAPTER SEVENTEEN

Our guest quarters are super swanky.

A room for the girls. A room for the boys. And a big bathroom in the middle.

With an oversize grease bath. I have only three words: Ew. That's narsty.

"We should get a good night's sleep and depart first thing in the morning," says Pan.

Moxie, Sparkles, and Seraphim dump their stuff in a pile on the floor.

"Well, if we're leaving tomorrow, we should stock up on food and supplies," says Moxie. "Who knows how long we'll be in these mountains." She turns to Knock-Knock, who is helping us get settled in. "Is there anywhere we can buy some stuff, Knock-Knock?"

The snome nods. "Yeppy-yep. Come-come. I will take-a you speedy-quick."

"Take us where?" asks Pan.

"I take-a you," she says again. "To the Hub."

The Hub is a riot of snome sights and sounds. Part marketplace, part swap meet, part demolition derby. It's bursting with sheet-metal stalls and makeshift stores. Smoke and steam fills the street. Clanking and rattling and small explosions echo from every corner.

I immediately think of market day in Conklin. Of checking out the newest arrivals at Wynchester's Weapons Emporium. One of my favorite pastimes. Window-shopping with Moxie.

"Moxie!" I cry. "Are you thinking what I'm thinking?"

"Window-shopping!" she cheers. "I've never been to a snome armory before. I wonder if they sell steam-powered war hammers!"

Seraphim steps up and places a tattooed hand on my shoulder. "Fart! Your rescuer has arrived!"

"What?" I'm confused.

"I know how boys are about shopping," she says. "Plus I need arrows. Consider yourself free."

"But . . ." I sputter.

"Seraphim, Knight of the Rose, wants to go window-shopping? With me?" cries Moxie, giddy at the thought. "That's so . . . fierce!"

"B-but . . ." I stammer.

"No need to thank me, Fart!" says Seraphim. "Take the afternoon off!"

Sparkles shakes her mane enthusiastically. "Don't think you're leaving me behind, ladies," she cheers. "I can shop until all of you drop. Come on, Pan. Girl date!"

"B-b-but . . ." I stutter.

"See you later, Fart!" Moxie cries over her shoulder.

I stand there and watch as the four of them stroll into the crowded streets. I can still see Seraphim and Sparkles above the heads of the snomes, laughing with Moxie and Pan. They turn a corner and disappear from sight.

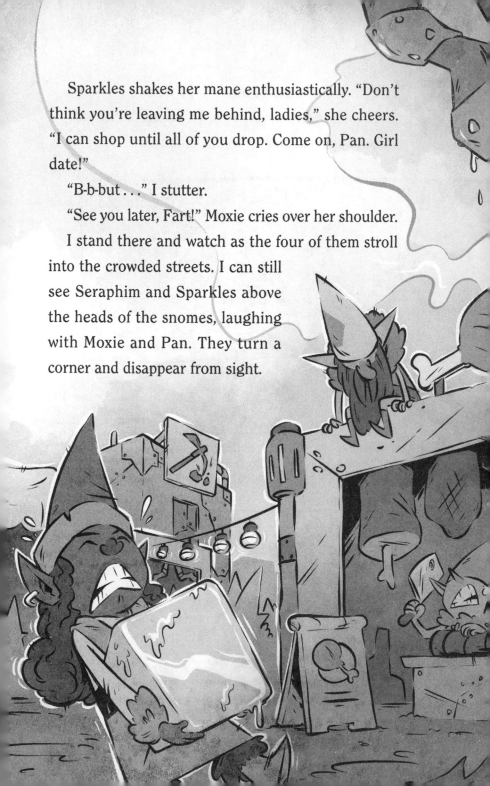

I sigh. Well, at least I have TickTock.

"Girls," I sneer. "Am I right, TickTock? TickTock?"

Then I spot him. With Knock-Knock.

Well. Looks like TickTock's found his soul mate. I'm happy for him.

"I guess it's just you and me, Bizzy," I say, turning to my bee. "Bizzy?"

I order a yeti-on-a-stick. I sit down. And I sigh.

I'm in a crowded marketplace. In a bustling snome city. The sounds of chatter and companionship are all around me.

Meanwhile . . . I've never felt so alone.

The suite is quiet when I get back. I guess I should be happy. I haven't had a room to myself in ages.

But the girls have left a mess behind. It's classic Moxie housekeeping. Bedrolls, backpacks, warrior weapons, spoonicorn saddle . . . it's all just tossed in the middle of the floor.

I grab the pile and hoist it into their room, dropping half of it on the way. I go back to gather up the spill, but the spoonicorn's saddlebags have leaked shroomie sporepods all over the floor. Not just shroomie sporepods. There's something else. The wanted posters.

I check the pockets of my robes. Nope. Gone.

Why would Sparkles take our wanted posters?

I unroll them.

Knight of the Rose seeks helpers for heroic quest. Neato.

Kidnapped! Prince Lockheed of Moltingvale. Whoop-de-do.

Wanted: The Arch Angel. Thievery, Robbery, Burglary, and Mischief. Wait a minute.

The thief in the poster looks so familiar. Gosh. Maybe it's one of the bandits that robbed us in Wetwater? I wonder . . .

But loud laughter knocks these thoughts from my mind. Apparently the shopping excursion was a success. I wouldn't know. But after four hours, the brave bargain hunters have returned triumphant, arms loaded with bags. I stuff the posters into my pocket and return to the other room.

"Fart!" cries Moxie, lugging something behind her. "Look what I got!"

It's a shield. The most enormous shield I've ever laid eyes on. Like, barn-door big.

"But you already have a shield," I point out. "And that one's almost taller than you are."

"I know." She shrugs sheepishly. "But Seraphim says a warrior's shield can never be too big!"

Well. If Seraphim says so.

Pan flumps down on one of the beds. "I've never really enjoyed shopping," she says. "But I must confess. That was fun." She lays her bo staff on the bed. Her brand-new bo staff.

"Where'd that come from?" I ask. "You already have a staff."

Seraphim chuckles. "You mean that piece of driftwood she was lugging around?"

Pan holds the staff out to me. I have to admit, it's gorgeous. Gnomish runes run around the end.

"Is this made from . . . glass?" I ask, lifting it effortlessly.

"Arkanium," says Moxie in awe. "Also known as clearstone. Gnomes love crafting things with it. Gosh, these little guys make neat weapons!"

ARKANIUM

Also known as "clearstone."

Clear as glass.

Light as a feather.

Hard as stone.

"Seraphim says this stone is the ideal material for a bo staff," Pan informs me. "Perfectly balanced."

Well. If Seraphim says so.

"Lightweight, yet strong as steel," says the knight with a crooked smile. "An extraordinary weapon for an extraordinary monk."

Pan flushes at the praise and turns away. "I'm going to go in the other room and have a rest," she says, taking the bo staff. "I'm exhausted."

"Same," says Seraphim, following her.

"Same," says Moxie.

"Hey, Moxie." I pull her aside. "How'd you guys pay for all this? I thought we were almost out of cash."

"Quit worrying, Little Wiz," she says, patting me reassuringly. "Seraphim says you have to spend money to make money."

Well. If Seraphim says so.

"Check this out, Banana Boy!" Sparkles walks into the room like a princess arriving at the ball. An iridescent scarf billows out from her neck. "It's made from plucked butterfly wings and the tears of naughty gnome children."

"Um . . . neat."

She tosses her mane. "It was expensive," she says. "But I think I'm worth it."

"Let me guess," I say. "Seraphim says it perfectly matches your eyes."

She shoots me a pouty look. "Aw. My Banana Boy. Don't hate me because I'm beautiful."

"Don't worry," I mutter. "That's not the main reason."

"Oh!" she says suddenly. "I got you something!" She starts rooting around in the pile of shopping bags. "Open your hand and close your eyes and I'll give you a big surprise."

I've faced owlbears and ogres. But this terrifies me more.

However, my curiosity gets the better of me. I do it. But if I open my eyes and there's a turd or something in my hand, well, I'll never trust again.

But when I open my eyes, it's not a turd. It's a shopping bag.

I reach in. I do not know how to describe what I pull out.

"Do you love it?" cries Spar-kles. "We can't all be fashion god-desses. I know this. So I do what I can to help where I'm needed."

RHINESTONE JUMPSUIT

"I'm not wearing this," I say flatly.

"Come on, Little Wiz! Those are real rhinestones!" she says with a squee. "You will look so rock star!"

"I'm not wearing this," I say again.

She shrugs. "Have it your way. If you want to walk around in that yard-sale housecoat looking like somebody's Aunt Gertrude, that's totally your choice." She tosses her head and goes to the other room.

Okay, it's possible I need a new set of robes. Maybe several sets.

But this? A rhinestone jumpsuit? With disco ball tassels?

I'm pretty sure this spoonicorn is just trying to make me look stupid.

Well, the joke's on her. Because I can look plenty stupid without any help from her, thank you very much.

CHAPTER EIGHTEEN

Gloomy.

That's the word for the next morning. Because dark clouds are gathering in the sky to the north. Also because we say goodbye to the snomes and head back out into the cold.

Boss-King Grease-Ratchet accompanies us to the front gate. Pan bows our thanks to him.

He pulls us close, like he wants to say something. He turns to Knock-Knock and starts to instruct the little snome. But then he waves her away. Stares at us. As if some things need to be said directly.

"Time," he mutters, the tall-talk words awkward in his mouth. "Time. Is. Key."

He reaches out and presses something into Pan's hand.

Sheesh. Grease-Ratchet has his own money.

Pan pats his hand. "I understand," she says. "Time is key. We'll try to hurry."

Then Knock-Knock leads us out into the towering drifts of snow. Bizzy and TickTock trail right behind her.

As we trudge, I pull Moxie and Pan aside.

"I need to talk to you guys," I tell them.

"What's up?" asks Moxie.

I'm not sure how to say it. So I just say it. "I don't trust that spoonicorn."

"Sparkles?" says Moxie with a snort.

"What makes you say this?" asks Pan soberly.

"I don't know," I admit. "Just a feeling. Like she's up to something."

"Up to something? *Sparkles?*" Moxie giggles. "She makes kitty-shaped sherbet pops come out of her head. How up-to-something can she be?"

"Are you sure it isn't because she calls you Banana Boy?" asks Pan.

"No," I say quickly. "Well, yes. But also I found these in her saddlebags." I show them the wanted posters.

Moxie shakes her head. "Why would Sparkles want our wanted posters?"

"I don't know!" I hiss.

"Perhaps you simply misplaced them," suggests Pan.

"I did not misplace them!"

Pan and Moxie glance at each other. We slog silently through the snow for a few moments. Then Pan speaks softly.

"I hear you," she says slowly. "However . . ." She hesitates. "Are you sure you're not just feeling a little bit . . . ?" She pauses again.

"What?" I ask. "Annoyed? Suspicious? Anti-spoonicorn? Yes. I'm feeling all those things."

Moxie cuts in. "She means are you sure you're not just . . ." She cringes and then says it. "Jealous?"

"Well, we've been spending a lot of time with Sparkles and Seraphim," Moxie says quickly. "It's a lot of girl energy."

"Exactly," says Pan softly. "Maybe there's nothing to be suspicious of at all. Perhaps you're simply feeling a little . . . left out."

"That's . . . that's . . . that's . . ." I have no words.

"We're just saying," Moxie says apprehensively. "Sparkles is the trusted companion of a Knight of the Rose."

"Agreed," says Pan reasonably. "She's a bit snarky. And oblivious. And she has the unfortunate habit of saying whatever pops into her head. But up to something? I have a hard time believing that."

Ugh. I hate it when Pan and Moxie make perfect sense. "Well, fine." I shrug. "Maybe so." I shake my head and follow Bizzy through a big snow drift. "But I'm not jealous," I hiss over my shoulder. "Not even close."

The thought is absolutely ridiculous. Laughable. Ludicrous.

And maybe a little true.

But still.

We continue to trudge. But the going is slow.

"I'm not sure we're ever going to get there with Tiny McSmallfry leading the way," Sparkles whispers, nodding at Knock-Knock. "No offense. I think she's super sweet and all. But this is taking, like, literally forever."

It's true. The drifts of snow are big, and Knock-Knock's legs are small. TickTock's not doing so hot either.

"You could give them a ride," I tell the spoonicorn. "Then they wouldn't have to walk."

She raises her eyebrows at me. "What do I look like? A horse?"

Actually, yes. Except for the weird spoon, she looks exactly like a horse.

"Please don't answer that," she says, cutting me off. "You'll only show your ignorance."

Seraphim turns to me. "Actually, it's a fantastic idea, Fart. Sincerely."

Sparkles rolls her eyes at the knight. "Excuse me? You know full well that I don't give out pony rides to just anybody. No offense."

"Not you," Seraphim assures her. "The bee."

Bizzy hovers effortlessly under their small weight, shooting me an uncertain look. "It's okay, girl," I say, rubbing her belly. "You give these guys a ride, okay?"

"That's what I'm talking about," says Sparkles. "Now maybe we'll get somewhere!"

For the next several hours, we make good time. Riding on Bizzy, Knock-Knock leads us over ridges. Around jutting rocks. On hidden paths through sparse evergreen trees that we never would have found on our own.

The gloomy clouds continue to gather, but they never dump their load of snow down on us. The wind howls harder than ever. We bundle our coats around us and keep climbing.

Up, up, up we clamber. After what seems like forever, we turn a bend. And there it is, looming before us.

The very top of the Frostflung Mountains.

But still no sign of a fortress.

"Where's Tinkertop?" I ask over the wind. "I thought it was at the top of the mountain?"

"You see-a soon-quick," says Knock-Knock. "Climb-a tip-top peak. Then see."

Bizzy weaves and bobs against the wind, shuttling her passengers quickly up the summit. But for the rest of us, it's slower going. Pan and Seraphim hop nimbly over the final jaggy crags like a couple of mountain goats. Sparkles makes her way daintily in their wake. Moxie clomps solidly right behind.

I crawl behind Moxie, pulling myself slowly up the final rise.

At the top, Pan and Moxie just stop and stare. Spellbound. Gazing into the distance.

I pull myself over the summit. I can't believe I made it.

SUPERHEROIC ACHIEVEMENT!
Mountain Climbing Master!
(350 Experience Points Awarded)

The wind whips my robes around me. Before us, the landscape sweeps away, a steep slope of untouched snow. It plummets for hundreds of feet before hitting a cluster of tall trees and vanishing over a cliff edge.

But it's what lies beyond that has everyone's jaws hanging open.

There's an island floating in the sky.

"Whoa," whispers Moxie.

"Wow," mutters the spoonicorn. She falls silent. For once, Sparkles the pompous pony is speechless.

"Wow is right," agrees Pan. "I have seen the elven kingdom of Kirajoy. I have seen the halls of Krakentop Academy. I have seen the wonders of Wetwater. But I have never seen anything like this."

The snome stronghold of Tinkertop.

"Tinkertop issa air island," says Knock-Knock proudly.

"What are those weird blobby birds?" asks Sparkles.

She's right. Flocks of strange chubby birds bob and weave slowly around the air island.

"Not birds," says Pan. Her sharp elf eyes squint into the distance. "Fish."

FLOAT-FISH

Not a blobby bird.
Fairly harmless to most humanoids.
Like a giant floating cow.
Primarily eats birds and large insects.

"Fish?" Moxie giggles. "That's silly!"

"No, elf be-a right," says Knock-Knock. "Be-a float-fish!"

"Are they dangerous?" I ask nervously.

"Not unless you-a birdy," replies Knock-Knock. "Then chomp-a fast-quick."

Seraphim steps forward, shielding her eyes from the sun. "We have a bigger problem than float-fish," says the knight. "How are we going to get to the island?"

She's right. At least half a mile of open air lies between us and the island.

"Don't know," says Knock-Knock. "Snomes use airships. But don't gotta none no more. Maybe tall-ones gotta magic flying horsey or something?"

"Nope," I say. "Our magic horsey only makes sherbet pops and hurtful words."

Behind me, Sparkles says nothing. But snow and pebbles tumble down on me.

"Cut it out, Sparkles," I tell her.

"I didn't do it," she cries defensively.

I turn. She turns. We all turn. And we see it. It's not the spoonicorn disturbing the snow at the top of the peak.

It's a yeti.

The yeti. The one from
the gondola. And he looks seriously cheesed off about the spanking we
gave him.

And crud on a cracker. He brought some buddies.

CHAPTER NINETEEN

One yeti almost made me piddle a puddle.

Two yetis is enough to make me boom-boom in my boxers.

But three?

Let's just say I'm gonna need new underpants when this is over.

Seraphim unleashes a firestorm of arrows at the big one. But they bounce off his pelt just like last time.

With a quick *"Pew-pew-patchoo!"* I fling a barrage of Magic Missiles at the beasts. Same deal. They just fizzle in their fur.

All three yetis let out bloodcurdling bellows and climb over the ridge, right at us.

"SERAPHIM!" roars Moxie. "GET EVERYONE OUT OF HERE!"

Pan starts to protest. "Moxie! Don't—"

"NOW!" Moxie cries, raising her big barn-door shield against the oncoming creatures. "I'll hold them off as long as I can! GO!"

"She's right," yells Seraphim grimly. "Come on!"

The knight jumps on Sparkles and tears furiously through the snow, down the hill, away from the yetis. But there's something this knight doesn't know: Pan and Moxie are the ham to my cheese. The hot fudge to my sundae. The tots to my taters. And together we are unbeatable.

"Pan!" I shout. "Death by Pebble!" I launch a Magic Missile into a nearby boulder. But the exploding gravel just falls to the ground. A whole lotta pebble. But no death.

I turn. And I see why. Because Pan isn't with me. She's with Seraphim.

The elf skitters down the hill after the knight. Bizzy, Knock-Knock, and TickTock trail in their wake.

Leaving me hamless. Hot-fudgeless. Totless. And very, very . . . beatable.

"Come on, Fart!" Pan cries up to me.

Moxie slams hammer against shield, drawing the attention of the thirty-foot monsters. She circles the yetis like a wrestler, turning them away from us so we can make our escape. "GO, FART!" Moxie roars, seeing me lingering. "NOW!"

The yetis fan out, cornering her against the summit like a rooster trapped on a rooftop.

Moxie is right. Seraphim is right. There's nothing I can do. I turn and flee down the hill after the others.

We huff and puff through the waist-high snow. But there's nowhere to go. Even if we make it to the bottom of the steep slope, there's nothing but a sheer drop-off waiting once we get there.

RAAAAAWWWWWWR!

The head yeti claws at Moxie, leaving a trail of nasty scratches on her shiny new shield.

"MOXIE!" I scream. At my cry, the other two yetis turn. They spot the rest of us stumbling down the hill. And they start shambling after us.

Moxie grabs her shield, angrily examining the gouges. The yeti lunges with fangs bared.

Enraged, Moxie swings her shield, slamming the huge creature across his furry face.

The yeti teeters, dazed by the pummeling.

The other two lumber toward us. Gaining. Like, speedy-quick.

Gritting her teeth, Moxie pulls her shield against her chest. And she leaps.

WHOOSH!

She hits the snow, using her shield as a sled. She's suddenly swooshing and slooshing down the hill at breakneck speed. Moxie the bobsledder.

Steering her shield-sled through the yetis' legs, Moxie sends them toppling into the snow. But it doesn't take them long to get it together. In three seconds flat, all three yetis are charging down the hill in angry pursuit. And dang, they are fast.

But not as fast as Moxie.

"Look out, Fart!" she yells.

WHAMMO!

She slams into me, knocking me off my feet. I tumble. Bumble. And crash. Right onto her shield.

We careen out of control, right at Pan. At the last possible second, she leaps. Backflipping through the air, she lands next to me like some pointy-eared spider monkey.

"Look out, Sparkles!" cries Moxie.

"*You* look out!" screams the spoonicorn.

WHA-BLAMMO!

We are jetting recklessly down a mountainside. Angry yetis are chasing us.

And I have spoonicorn butt in my face. For your information, it doesn't smell as much like rainbows as you might imagine. Mostly it smells like horse heinie.

You know what else is bonkers? The cliff. The one we're heading right for.

Moxie digs her hammer into the snow behind us, trying desperately to slow us down.

"Brakes!" screams Sparkles. "Hit the brakes!"

"Working on it!" says Moxie. She's kicking up a sheet of slush behind us. But we're not slowing down.

"Fart!" Pan cries. "I need fire!"

That's all she has to say. I know exactly how to respond.

"*Flimmity-flamesh!*" I cry, casting Cozy Camp and sending a small spark into the air before me. Pan mutters some chant to the elements and breathes life into the flickering flame. It quickly becomes a blazing fountain of fire that shoots from her hands into the snow before us.

The air hisses with steam as the snow sizzles and melts.

We're a hundred feet from the edge of oblivion.

With a path melted, Moxie's hammer finally makes contact with rock. A shrill screech fills the air as silver scrapes on stone.

SCREEEEEEEECH!

Fifty feet from plummeting to our deaths.

SCREEEEEEEECH!

Twenty-five.

Ten.

I close my eyes and say my prayers. The shield shudders to a grinding halt.

We've stopped. Inches from the edge.

SUPERHEROIC ACHIEVEMENT!
Shield Sledding Success!
(350 Experience Points Awarded)

Seraphim and Sparkles clamber off the shield. "That was fun!" says Seraphim.

"That was not fun," says Sparkles, looking queasy. "That was nauseating. And possibly gave me a crick in my neck. I may be filing a lawsuit against the manufacturer of that ride."

Bizzy flutters nearby, with Knock-Knock and Tick-Tock holding tightly to fistfuls of fuzz. "Not being out of this yet!" TickTock cries, pointing. "Look!"

The yetis are halfway down the hill and coming fast. We haven't escaped. We've only delayed our doom.

"We'll have to fight," Moxie says, pulling her scraped and scratched shield onto her arm. "There's nowhere else to go."

"TickTock! Knock-Knock! Get out of here!" I cry. "There's no sense in all of us dying."

"Not again!" cries TickTock. "TickTock is not going to do running away and leaving friends behind!"

"There's nothing you can do," says Pan solemnly. She crouches low, readying her bo staff as the furious yetis barrel toward us.

"Tall-ones!" cries Knock-Knock. "Getta onna buzzy bee speedy-quick! We fly away!"

"No room!" I shout. I swat my bee on the rump. "Bizzy! Go!"

She flutters away obediently, taking Knock-Knock and TickTock out over open space, far from reach.

The rest of us turn to face the yetis.

So nobody sees it when the float-fish attack.

CHAPTER TWENTY

When jumbo puffer fish attack, it's never a pleasant sight.

But when they try to eat your bee? Well, it's downright upsetting.

Most of the float-fish hover out near the air island. But one has caught sight of Bizzy. And it seems to have only one thought:

Bee. It's what's for dinner.

Knock-Knock spots it just in time. "Looky out, buzzy bee!" she cries. She grabs a fistful of bee fluff and steers sharply down, just missing the fish's gulping mouth.

"Bizzy!" I cry.

"TickTock!" Pan yells.

"Little gnome girl whose name I can't remember!" screeches Sparkles.

"Quit worrying about them," Seraphim says. She points at the yetis thundering toward us. "We've got problems of our own."

Sheesh. Harsh. I mean, yes, we do have problems of our own. But still. Sheesh.

As we turn back to the charging yetis, the knight raises her bow and takes careful aim.

TWANG!

The bowstring flies, sending its arrow into a yeti eye socket. The beast shrieks in pain, collapsing in an explosion of snow.

"Go for the eyes," the knight tells us. "It's our only chance."

The wounded yeti rises to its feet. Releasing a furious roar, it yanks out the arrow, crumples it to kindling, and keeps on coming.

The creatures are closing fast. But my attention is on my bee. More float-fish have noticed her. They bob after her, eager to gulp down this buzzy little bonbon.

She leads them on a merry chase, a chain of puffy fish trailing in her wake.

And watching the parade of float-fish that dip and dive after her, I see it. Our way out.

I let out a loud whistle. Bizzy hears it immediately. She abruptly changes course. Barely missing the chomping jaws of the floating fish behind her, she zips back toward the cliff. Toward us.

"Knock-Knock!" I cry, pointing at the cliff edge. "Under! Fly *under*!"

The little snome holds on for dear life, confusion and fear on her face. "Under?"

And then understanding dawns on her. "Under!" she cries. "Got it!" She spurs Bizzy with her heels. TickTock holds on tightly as they shoot down, below the cliff edge and out of sight, float-fish hungrily trailing behind.

Seraphim fires another arrow. But these yetis aren't as dumb as they look. The creature swipes the arrow with a leathery hand, sending it bouncing harmlessly into the snow.

Moxie grips and ungrips her hammer nervously. The yetis are less than fifty feet away and closing. Pan twirls her arkanium bo staff, ready to give the creatures a beatdown or die trying.

"Put away your weapons," I tell them. "We can't fight these guys."

"Oh my gosh!" says Sparkles in a panic. "What do you want us to do? Sing them a song?"

"Maybe later," I say. My eyes are peeled, watching for Bizzy. Then I spot her. She's doing a flyby, passing just under the cliff edge. A line of float-fish still trail hungrily behind her.

"For now," I tell my friends, "just follow me."

And I jump off the cliff.

I land with a *BOING* on the back of the first float-fish. Its bouncy-castle body sends me slipping, but I grab one of its spiky spines and hold on tight.

Pan is the first to latch on to my idea. She takes the leap, landing nimbly on to the next float-fish. Seraphim follows, trailed closely by Sparkles.

Only Moxie remains. Our train of float-fish is leaving the station, with only three fish left. Then two.

I watch terrified as the yetis lunge at Moxie, claws raised, fangs dripping with froth. But then, at the last

possible second, Moxie leaps. She slams onto the last fish. Bounces once. Bounces twice. Starts to slip and slide off into the miles-long drop below.

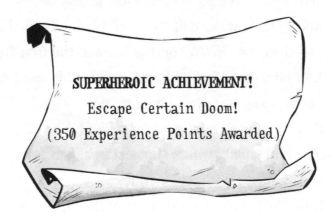

SUPERHEROIC ACHIEVEMENT!
Escape Certain Doom!
(350 Experience Points Awarded)

The yetis skitter to a stop at the cliff edge, screaming furiously into the void as we fly off into the sunset.

CHAPTER TWENTY-ONE

Tinkertop glitters before us like a crown in the fading sunlight.

One thing about float-fish. They are determined but not very fast. Or smart. They don't seem to notice that they've acquired some uninvited passengers.

As we approach, the glaring sunset passes behind the air island, and we see the fortress as it really is.

Ruined. Neglected. Abandoned.

Attacked. By Glacierbane.

Even now there's a whisper of smoke wafting up from the hole. As if the dragon sleeps just inside.

From my perch on the lead float-fish, I spot an

overgrown courtyard at the front of the fortress. And near it, a massive gate.

"Front door, Knock-Knock!" I cry, pointing. "Front door!"

"Got it! Speedy-quick!" she screeches back.

The snome loops Bizzy low and slow through the courtyard, the float-fish trailing steadily behind. One by one, we hop off.

Special delivery. We couldn't get any closer if these fish put stamps on our foreheads and pushed us through the mail slot.

Hole in roof.

Scorch marks.

Us on float-fish.

Weeds.

Stained.

SUPERHEROIC ACHIEVEMENT!
Ride a Fish!
(300 Experience Points Awarded)

But there's no time to celebrate. "Fish won't stop chasing!" TickTock calls down to us. His voice echoes alarmingly off the turrets of the abandoned stronghold.

"You'll have to lose them, Knock-Knock," says Pan.

Knock-Knock zigs, but the float-fish follow. Knock-Knock zags, but still she can't shake the mob of hungry swimmers trailing behind them.

TickTock points out a small moss-covered archway. Nodding, Knock-Knock turns Bizzy and pilots her through the arch, her round body barely clearing the sides. The fish try to follow, but it's like cramming a balloon through a keyhole.

By the time they unclog themselves from the archway, their yummy-time bee snack has disappeared. Disappointed, they scatter to rejoin their flock, probably dreaming of easier meals. Or slower bees.

Knock-Knock, TickTock, and Bizzy emerge from behind a tower and buzz down to us.

"Nice flying, Knock-Knock!" Moxie cheers, clapping her on the back.

"Is like-a airship!" says the little snome. "Really small bobbly airship!"

I run to Bizzy and rub her belly proudly. "Who's a clever bee? Who is? WHO IS?"

"Indeed, Fart," agrees Pan. "That escape idea was inspired."

"Yes!" says Knock-Knock, grabbing my big hand in her tiny one. "I thought-a tall-ones were yeti bait for sure!"

I soak in the praise and take a look around.

The courtyard is overgrown with weeds and roots. Bent trees grow through shattered cobblestones. A statue of a gnome towers nearby. No, not just a gnome. It's Boss-King Grease-Ratchet. The guy has his own money *and* his own statue. He stands proudly before the front gate, pointing into the distant mountaintops.

But there's no time to sightsee. Sparkles has already discovered a problem. "Um . . . guys," she says, hoof thrust toward the mountain peaks. "How are we ever going to get back when the time comes? We are literally trapped."

"I got you, sis," says Seraphim. The knight pulls out a long length of slender rope and ties it to an arrow. Taking careful aim, she fires through the void.

The arrow hits home, burying itself into one of the trees that dot the far mountainside. Seraphim ties the other end of the rope to a gnarled tree nearby.

"Homemade zip line," she says, flashing a jaunty smile.

"I seeya the workshop when we fly around," says Knock-Knock. "At back-a of fortress."

"Perfect," says Moxie. "You and TickTock can take Bizzy and go find Grease-Ratchet's bot."

"Yes," says Pan, nodding. "But keep silent. With any luck, Glacierbane will be sleeping. We can slip in, grab what we need, and get out before the dragon knows we're here."

"Okay," says the little phibling. "TickTock and Knock-Knock meet you back here once we are being done!" Bizzy flickers her wings, carrying the snome and the phibling around a tower and out of sight.

Before us looms the gate of Tinkertop. But it's like no gate I've ever seen.

"No keyhole to pick," points out Seraphim. "No lock. No handle. No knob."

Moxie runs her fingers along it. "How do you think we get in?"

Pan examines it thoughtfully. "Remember the door to Grease-Ratchet's bathhouse?" she reminds us.

"Yeah," says Moxie with a nod. "It had all those levers and dials."

"Precisely," says Pan. "Gnome-constructed. No doubt there will be some hidden lever or mechanism that activates this gate. We simply have to find it."

We spread out and begin searching the courtyard. We pull torch brackets. Push loose stones. Paw the walls and tug on rivets. But nothing gets the mysterious door to budge.

Soon we've exhausted all options. Aside from weeds, vines, and the statue of Boss-King Grease-Ratchet, the courtyard is empty.

Sparkles flops down next to the statue. "You'd think boss man greaseball could at least give us a hint," she says in frustration.

"Hint!" says Pan excitedly. She fishes out the gear-shaped coin that Grease-Ratchet handed to her before we left. "He did give us a hint. Look!"

She holds out the coin. There, engraved cleverly into the metal, is the image of the boss-king. Like the statue, the little Grease-Ratchet on the coin points off into space with one hand. In the other it holds something aloft. A lantern.

No . . . an hourglass.

And so does the statue.

"Quick!" cries Pan excitedly. "Search the statue!"

Moxie peels away the weeds and vines that cover the statue's base. Once cleared off, we see that the statue stands on a circular podium. Embedded into the podium, circling the statue like the numbers on a clock, are seven gold symbols.

"Look at these!" says Moxie eagerly. "A tree. A sundial. A candle."

"A moon," I say, examining the symbols closely. "A bird. A flower. And a little guy."

"Oh my gosh!" Sparkles says. "You guys! I bet this totally *means* something!"

Pan nods. "Yes. It's obviously some type of mechanism. We just need to figure out how to trigger it."

Sparkles clops over to a mossy spot and flops down. "No offense, guys. But that could take forever. Like, I could seriously chew a rock into a key with my teeth before we figure that out."

"Key!" I say. "That's it! Pan, what was it that Grease-Ratchet said to you when he gave you the coin? Right before we left?"

"Time is key," says Pan.

"He was just telling us to hurry, Banana Boy," says Sparkles. "The guy wants his battle-bot."

"No he wasn't!" I shout with realization. "He was telling—"

"I've got it!" Seraphim says, cutting me off. "He was telling us how to open the door! Time is the key!"

"Yes! Of course!" cries Pan. "The statue of Grease-Ratchet holds an hourglass! A measurement of time! You're brilliant, Seraphim!"

Seraphim is brilliant? No. *Fart* is brilliant! I was the one who thought of it before Archer McInterruption-Face cut me off. But nobody else seems to notice.

Pan races around the pedestal, examining the little symbols. "Each of these things . . . they each last for a specific amount of time. A sundial measures a single day. The moon goes through its full cycle every month. A flower lasts for only a season before its bloom fades away."

"It's a combination lock!" says Moxie. "We turn the statue to aim the gnome's finger at the right symbol!"

"In the order of how long they last!" says Pan excitedly.

Seraphim examines the symbols. "Well, a candle burns for only a few hours, so that would be the shortest."

I knew that. But why bother sharing? Seraphim will just get credit for it.

"Then the sundial, which measures a day," adds Pan.

"Then the moon, which lasts a month before starting over," joins in Moxie.

"Then what?" asks Seraphim. "The bird? The tree?"

"The flower," says Pan with certainty. "It blooms for a season. Then the bird. A raven lives for about ten to fifteen years."

"Fine, what next?" I ask. "The tree? Or the guy?"

"Well, a tree lives longer than a human," notes Seraphim. "Trees can live for hundreds of years."

"Yes, that's true," says Pan. "But why would the gnomes put a picture of a human on their lock?" She examines the little engraving closely. "No, my guess is that this symbol is a gnome. And gnomes, like elves, can live for thousands of years. Which means the tree comes next and then the gnome."

"So that's the combination!" cries Moxie. "Candle-sundial-moon-flower-raven-tree-gnome!"

Seraphim and Moxie grab the statue, muscles bulging as they tug it toward the candle.

No luck. It doesn't budge.

Moxie lets go, panting for breath. "Maybe we're wrong."

"No," says Pan stubbornly. "I'm certain this is right."

LOOKIE HERE!

And then it hits me. "Time is key!" I reach out and take the gear-shaped coin from Pan. I search the statue, pawing at every little crack and crevice. And then I spot it. Under the hourglass.

I insert the gear into the slot. I turn it. There's a satisfying click.

"Now try it," I say, stepping away from the statue.

Moxie grips the base of the statue. And pulls.

The statue swivels freely, unlocked, turning in place like a dial. Moxie shoots us an excited grin and begins to line up the arm of the statue.

"Candle, sundial, moon." Moxie lines up each symbol in their turn. At every symbol, the statue lets out a loud click, as if locking the combination into place. "Flower, raven, tree." She looks at us with anticipation and swivels the statue a final time. "Gnome."

KKRRRIIIIIIIICCKK!

We hear the grinding of rusty metal from behind us. The spiral mechanisms of the door slide out of the way.

The door to Tinkertop is open.

SUPERHEROIC ACHIEVEMENT!
Solve a Tricky Combination Lock!
(350 Experience Points Awarded)

We stare at the door. Nobody moves. Fingers of smoke billow softly from the opening. And a smell. A sour, sickening smell.

It is the smell of evil. Of dragon. Of Glacierbane.

Seraphim readies her bow. Moxie white-knuckles her hammer. Pan sweeps stray hair-wispies from her face. Sparkles sets her jaw ferociously.

And I mentally kiss my butt goodbye.

We step forward one by one. And we enter the dragon's lair.

CHAPTER TWENTY-TWO

The first thing we notice is the heat. An unnatural warmth. Like all of Tinkertop is being heated by some unseen fire.

Dragon fire.

According to *Buzzlock's Big Book of Beasts*:

1) Dragons . . . live for thousands of years.

Like elves. Or gnomes. But unlike elves and gnomes, dragons are evil, powerful, and, thankfully, incredibly rare.

2) Dragons . . . love treasure.

Above all else. They'll usually find a fortress or a cave where there's a lot of good loot already and then add to it, building up their horde of riches.

3) Dragons . . . have hordewrath.

They instinctively know every ounce of their treasure, down to a single coin. If one copper piece is pilfered from their pile, they know it instantly. This allows them to ferociously protect their treasure.

4) Dragons . . . breathe fire.

In spite of all the stories you may have heard about heroes that slay dragons, actually slaying one is super difficult. Anyone who tries almost always learns this the hard way. When intruders are discovered, a dragon destroys them with its fiery breath or simply gobbles them up whole.

And when it's not gathering more treasure or gobbling down dumb heroes . . .

5) Dragons . . .
sleep.

Stretched out on a mountain of treasure like a lazy cat in the afternoon sun.

I desperately hope we can get in and out before kitty knows we're here.

We pass through the main gate into a grand entrance hall. Tattered tapestries cover the walls. Faded banners trimmed in yeti fur hang from above, flanking an enormous arch that opens into the city itself.

Meanwhile was impressive. But Tinkertop is next-level.

As the setting sun paints long shadows across the snomish city, it's hard for me to take in the beauty of this place.

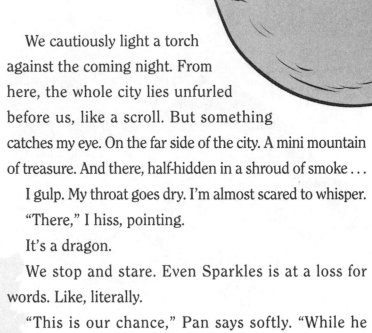

We cautiously light a torch against the coming night. From here, the whole city lies unfurled before us, like a scroll. But something catches my eye. On the far side of the city. A mini mountain of treasure. And there, half-hidden in a shroud of smoke . . .

I gulp. My throat goes dry. I'm almost scared to whisper.

"There," I hiss, pointing.

It's a dragon.

We stop and stare. Even Sparkles is at a loss for words. Like, literally.

"This is our chance," Pan says softly. "While he sleeps. Find what we need, get it, and get out."

We step slowly forward. But Pan pauses and glances at the knight.

Pan has made it clear that she's embarrassed by the poop part of our mission. How we're supposed to execute Project Pooper-Scooper without Sparkles and Seraphim seeing is beyond me.

But, as always, Pan has a plan. "Will you and Sparkles stay here?" she asks the knight. "Keep watch?"

Seraphim nods. "I like your style, sis. Guard the way out." She gives us a thumbs-up.

Shooting them a nervous final look, Pan, Moxie, and I creep slowly down the deserted streets of Tinkertop. We carefully avoid the treasure. Every step we take seems to echo loudly through the empty streets. But the dragon dozes on.

We turn a corner and delve deeper into the city. Soon we're in among the buildings, the dragon lost from sight.

"Keep your eyes peeled for poo piles," says Moxie. "They should be easy enough to spot. That dragon is huge."

True enough. And yet, hour after hour, street after street, alley after alley, the place is completely poop-less.

Sneaking down a darkened side street, we are flanked on all sides by crumbling stone and rotting debris. Suddenly from among the rubble comes a scuttling sound.

A caterpillar-like creature emerges, easily eight feet long. Dozens of legs writhe and scurry. Several long wavy feelers lash the air before it, searching, feeling, flaying.

"Oh, grody," says Moxie, raising her shield. "A filth feaster."

FILTH FEASTER

Feeds on the waste of animals—mostly eats poop.

Also called the cleaner of the dungeon.

The critter stares at us with its bulbous buggy eyes. Its mouthparts move furiously, clicking and clacking.

Moxie moves forward, hammer ready to bug-bash.

"Wait," I say, stopping her. "Hold it."

"Hold it?" says Moxie, taken aback. "I'm the resident bug-crusher. Why would I hold it?"

Pan raises her hand. "Fart is right. Any battle will be certain to make noise and could rouse the dragon."

"Yeah, but that's not what I mean," I say. "Remember the water weirdo?"

"Right," says Moxie. "Another poo muncher, like this one."

"Exactly," I say. "And since poo is what we seek, who better to talk to than the local poo muncher?"

"Talk to it?" she says. "But it's just a monster."

Pan nods approvingly. "Things are not always as they seem," she says with a smirk. "Fart. Proceed."

I never planned on chatting up so many creepy-crawlies. But Magic Mouth is turning out to be a handy spell.

I whisper the incantation. *"Sprechital linguoso!"* Suddenly the creature's chittering noises become words to my ears.

"... been forever since anybody's had the nerve to come in here," the filth feaster clicks, "and boy-oh-boy, that means Anton is gonna eat good at long last. 'Cuz bird droppings and float-fish scat just ain't cutting the mustard, you know what I mean?"

Anton the filth feaster. Sure. Why not?

I raise my hands in what I hope is a universal symbol of peace. "Hold it, hold it," I tell the creature. "Your name is Anton?"

"Well, well," says the filth feaster. "Looky-looky who can talk the talk and walk the walk. Hey, you got any food on you, two-legger?"

I reach into my pockets. "I think I've got some yeti jerky."

But the creature makes a face of disgust. "Gross. When I say 'food,' I'm talking primo poo. Grade A number two. Cream-of-the-crop crapola."

I wince in disgust. "Ah, no. Actually, we're kind of looking for some dragon doody ourselves."

"Well, good luck with that," says Anton. "Any dragon doo around here got eaten up or dried to dust long ago. It's been ages since this lizard has laid fresh logs."

"Um . . . why is that?" I ask.

"Boy, you're not too slick, are you, slick? In order to poo, you gotta om-nom. Can't do the one without the other. And this dragon ain't eaten in years. No food, no feces. That's how it works."

I relay Anton's message to Pan and Moxie. Pan nods in frustration. "Of course, it makes complete sense. It's probably been decades since any heroes ventured in here to try to slay Glacierbane. He hasn't eaten anyone in all that time. Which means our quest is hopeless."

"Well, that's just great," mutters Moxie. "No dragon poop, no dragon-digested magic item. What are we going to do now?"

But neither of us gets a chance to answer. Because suddenly the air explodes with a sound that turns our blood to ice.

RRRRRROOOOOOOOOOOAAAAAAAAAR!

"Oh boy," says Anton the filth feaster. "That's as good as the dinner bell. Hey, if I'm eating you in poop form this time tomorrow, it's nothing personal!" And with that, Anton burrows through a hole in the rubble and disappears from sight.

A voice like an avalanche splits the air, rattling the very foundation of the snome fortress.

Glacierbane . . . is awake.

"THIEVES!" the voice roars. "TREACHEROUS VILLAINS! PETULANT SCUM! HOW DARE YOU INVADE THE SANCTITY OF MY LAIR?! HOW DARE YOU TOUCH WHAT IS MINE?!"

Pan rounds on me. "Fart! Kevin told us not to touch the treasure! What did you do?"

"It wasn't me!" I cry innocently, holding out my empty hands.

Pan's eyes dart to Moxie.

"I didn't do it!" chokes the dwarf, her face pale with fear.

We turn and sprint down the street. Away from the sound of the dragon. Back to the exit.

Running hard, I hear the sound of wingbeats. I sneak a peek over my shoulder.

The dragon has taken to the air. His wings are like a hurricane, sending smoke, dust, and gold everywhere. But that's not what fills me with terror.

It's his eyes.

They glitter with hatred, searching the streets for intruders. And they land right on us.

We've been spotted.

"MISERABLE CREATURES!" he roars. "WORTHLESS WORMS! YOU WILL BE CRUSHED AND CRISPED BY THE FIRE AND FURY OF GLACIERBANE!"

"Dang it!" says Moxie, dashing under an awning as we tear up the street. "This was supposed to be a simple smash-and-grab! How did he hear us?"

"I have no idea," Pan shoots over her shoulder. "We were so careful not to touch the treasure."

We cross a short bridge spanning a treasure-flooded canal and round a corner. There before us looms the huge archway. The way out.

But that's not all.

Standing near a pile of dragon gold is the world's most punchable pony. Sparkles.

Stupid spoonicorn.

"Sparkles!" I shout. "You know you can't take this treasure! It's protected by hordewrath!"

The spoonicorn rounds on me. "I didn't take anything, Banana Boy! Do I look like I have hands? Or pockets?"

"Then who did it?!" I cry. "Who touched the treasure?!"

Sparkles shakes her mane indignantly and trots out of the way.

And there, bags overflowing with gold, jewels, and other assorted dragon loot . . . is Seraphim.

CHAPTER TWENTY-THREE

Glacierbane is coming for us.

We should be fleeing for our lives. We should be running for cover. We should be pooping our pants.

But all we can do is stare at Seraphim.

"What . . . ?" says Pan.

"Why . . . ?" says Moxie.

"You . . . ?" says me.

But there's no time for one-word questions.

Flames explode around us. The arched entry hall looms tantalizingly close. As the flames recede, I muster my courage and make a dash for it. I feel the snap of dragon jaws at my trailing robes. But suddenly Pan

slams her arkanium bo staff into the beast's snout, pole-vaulting over it and freeing the way for escape.

All of us barrel through the archway, diving for cover among the falling banners and fluttering tapestries.

"WRETCHED DOGS!" roars the dragon. "SNIVEL-ING INSECTS! YOU WILL TASTE THE TEMPEST OF MY VENGEANCE!" The beast slams the weight of his body against the wall behind us. But the snome-built walls hold.

We're safe for the moment. A fur-trimmed banner flutters from the wall, landing on Seraphim. The fur blankets the knight's pink hair like a shaggy white wig. Something about it seems so familiar.

And then it all clicks. I fish in my pockets and remove the wanted poster.

The Arch Angel . . . I couldn't place where I'd seen that face before. But now I do. Under that shock of long white hair . . . is a familiar crooked smile.

It's Seraphim.

I whirl on her. "This!" I cry, showing the poster.

"This is you!"

"Fart, snap out of it," Seraphim shouts, pushing past me. "You're delirious with dragon fear. Come on, guys. Let's vamoose while we still can!"

BLAMM! The dragon slams the walls behind us. But they hold.

"She's not a knight at all!" I cry to Moxie and Pan. "Seraphim ... is the Arch Angel!"

"Oh, Fart," says Seraphim. "Listen to yourself. You're just jealous of my new friendship with Pan and Moxie."

I struggle to find words. "That's ... that's not ..."

Seraphim raises a cocky eyebrow at me. "Admit it. You'll say anything to break up our little girl gang. It's really sad."

"Fart!" Pan cries. "I know you feel left out, but now is not the time or place!"

"Yeah, come on, man," says Moxie. "Seriously."

"But ..." I sputter.

BLAMM! The walls shudder again.

I grab Pan and Moxie and hold the poster in front of their faces. "Will you just look?! This is why she stole the wanted posters from me! She didn't want me to recognize her! *This* is Seraphim!"

Pan grabs the poster and stares at Seraphim. "The hair is shorter. And pink now." But then a look of realization crosses her elven features like a storm cloud. "However, there is no mistaking that smile."

Seraphim's face falls for just a second. But then the mask of confidence and charm is back. "Don't be ridiculous, Pan. I am a knight! A Knight of the . . . thingy . . ." Her eyes dart down to the emblem on her armor.

"What?!" cries Moxie. "*Thingy?* You're a Knight of the Rose! It's emblazoned on your armor for crying out loud!"

BLAMM! Dust and debris shower us from the ceiling.

But I don't care. "The only reason she came with us was to get a shot at the dragon's treasure!" I roar.

Seraphim sighs sadly. She pulls out an arrow. And draws her bow. "Bull's-eye," she says with a tight grin. "You got me. I gotta say, Little Wiz. You really are much more clever than you look."

BLAMMO!

The wall suddenly gives way. A scaly red snout bursts through the crumbling stone, scorching the entry hall with embers and smoke.

"LIARS!" roars Glacierbane. "THIEVES! SCOUNDRELS! YOU WILL BURN!"

Chaos and confusion explode into the chamber. And, in that moment, Seraphim the Arch Angel . . . runs. Darting through the entry hall, she dashes for the front gate, the spoonicorn galloping in her wake.

We tear after her, the heat of dragon breath licking our heels.

We dive through the opening and throw ourselves to the side just as the massive red snout snaps through the circular gate.

The bronze walls shudder as Glacierbane throws his weight against them. But again the walls hold.

With a roar of fury and frustration the dragon unleashes a blast of dragon fire onto the courtyard. We cringe from the heat as it explodes outward, melting the statue of Grease-Ratchet into a pile of molten slag.

The snout disappears back into the fortress. The stronghold echoes with the clatter of the scrambling monster, seeking another way at us.

Our eyes scan the courtyard. And there at the far end are Seraphim and Sparkles.

By the rope. Our only lifeline back to the mountain. Our one way off this rock.

"You don't deserve to wear that armor!" Moxie yells, the sound of betrayal thick in her voice.

"Probably not," says Seraphim smoothly. "Since I stole it from a Knight of the Rose."

Pan shakes her head in disbelief. "How could you?!" she asks. "You pretended to be our friend! You've been using us the whole time!"

"Oh my gosh," says Sparkles with a snotty look. "If

you're going to cry about it, I'm fresh out of tissues. No offense."

Moxie grips her hammer, anger burning in her eyes.

But Seraphim's bow is out and aimed. "Don't do it, Moxie," she says, her voice steely. "You know I can shoot the tick off an owlbear's back at five hundred yards."

The clatter of destruction shatters the air. Somewhere, the dragon has burst from the building.

Seraphim shoulders her bow. Her hand reaches for the rope.

"Come on, Sera," says Sparkles, nudging the thief. "Let's get out of here. These losers can deal with the dragon."

Seraphim draws a cruelly curved dagger and casually holds it out at the spoonicorn. "It kills me to do this, Sparkles. Truly. But how are you supposed to hold on to the rope?" She points the dagger at the spoonicorn's hooves. "No hands. I'm afraid you'll only slow me down."

The spoonicorn snarls. "Why, you little . . ."

Seraphim waves the dagger at her. "Back. Just get back."

The spoonicorn grits her teeth and snorts in anger. But she backs up to join the rest of us.

The roar of the dragon echoes from somewhere on

the island. The thief takes that as her cue to exit. Coiling her hand around the rope, Seraphim places the dagger against it.

"Seraphim!" Pan drops her bo staff and holds her hands aloft. She approaches the thief, pleading in her voice. "We can find a way out of this together," she says. "You don't have to do this."

For a moment Seraphim looks truly torn. "Come with me!" she says suddenly. "There's room on this rope for three of us. You, me, Moxie! We make a great team!"

"No way!" cries Moxie, bristling with anger.

"Oh, come on, Moxie!" cries Seraphim, moving toward them. "Think about it, sis! The Arch Angels. Doing what we want. Taking what we want. Imagine the fun the three of us would have!"

Pan pauses, considering Seraphim's words. "That does seem like it would be fun," says Pan. Then her voice hardens. "But things are not always as they seem."

Seraphim's face falls. Hardens. But then, like a cloud passing over the sun, that familiar crooked smile returns. Gripping the rope tightly with one hand, Seraphim leans in and whispers to Pan, "That's true, Pan. That's very true."

And then she does it. It happens so fast my mind barely registers the significance.

Seraphim's free hand closes around Pan's necklace. Her mom's necklace. With a sharp tug, she yanks it from the elf's neck.

And then, with a *snick!* quicker than sight, she cuts the rope with her dagger.

"NO!" cries Pan, grabbing desperately for her necklace. But she's grasping at thin air.

The Arch Angel is gone.

CHAPTER TWENTY-FOUR

Seraphim swings through the sky toward the first rays of morning. Toward the looming mountainside. Toward freedom.

But suddenly the horizon, the sunrise, the very mountainside itself, are blotted out. The air is filled with fire. Death. Destruction.

And one really big lizard.

Glacierbane.

Even midswing, Seraphim somehow sends three arrows at the dragon. But they bounce from the dragon's scales like pesky gnats.

The dragon unleashes a surge of flame at Seraphim's

rope, burning it instantly away and sending the sneak thief plummeting to her doom.

But this girl is quick. Crafty. Annoyingly skilled.

Performing some crazy roll-and-tuck maneuver, she hooks her bow on one of the dragon's enormous toenails. She hoists herself up. And she begins climbing.

Glacierbane roars with fury at being clambered up like some schoolyard jungle gym. He twirls and turns in midair, trying to shake off the thief. But still Seraphim holds on.

RUN. Something in my brain screams for me to get out of there. Seek shelter. Pull a disappearing act. While the dragon is otherwise occupied.

But my feet are frozen. My eyes are glued to the deadly aerial ballet happening before me.

Using her free hand, Seraphim slashes at the back of the dragon's leg with her dagger, desperately searching for a tender spot. But Glacierbane is armored in bright red scales from tip to toe.

The dragon twirls again. The thief's dagger flies into oblivion as she grabs on tightly with both hands. And still Seraphim climbs.

"PESTILENT FLEA!" Glacierbane roars. "DON'T YOU KNOW WHO I AM?"

The dragon hurls himself against the sheer rock face, trying desperately to scrape off his unwanted passenger. But Seraphim leaps up the dragon's wing seconds before being crushed against the cliff face.

But Seraphim dares. She fires several arrows at the beast's wing.

The dragon howls in pain. Snarling, he manages to snatch Seraphim with his claw, plucking the thief from his shoulder and flinging her skyward like a rag doll.

Even as she sails through the air, Seraphim manages to send arrows raining down at the beast. Chin. Cheek. Nose. They all bounce off the diamond-hard hide.

The dragon swoops at the falling figure of the thief, jaws wide, letting out a bone-rattling roar that shakes the mountainside.

For a second, I see it. Seraphim looks our way, that familiar crooked smile still plastered confidently across her face. She winks in our direction. As if there's some secret that only she knows.

And then . . .

Just like that, Seraphim the Arch Angel . . . is gone.

CHAPTER TWENTY-FIVE

And they lived happily ever after.

How come I never get to say that at this part in the story? It's unfair, really.

Having swallowed the bow-wielding thief in one gulp, Glacierbane turns to the rest of his pest-control problem.

Better known as: us.

Better known as: yikes.

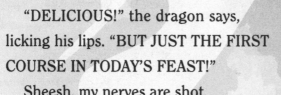

"DELICIOUS!" the dragon says, licking his lips. "BUT JUST THE FIRST COURSE IN TODAY'S FEAST!"

Sheesh, my nerves are shot.

Thankfully my feet are no longer frozen.

I run for safety through the front gate. I turn to see Moxie and Pan are right at my side. But there's no sign of the traitorous spoonicorn.

She's stuck. Like a rat in a trap. Her pink designer horseshoe is wedged between two roots.

Serves her right.

Nasty no-good liar. Pan, Moxie, and I look at one

another. There's a split second where I think we're actually going to do it. Leave her behind.

But that's just not who we are.

Stupid spoonicorn.

We dash from cover. Pan and Moxie grab her leg and yank, desperately trying to free the stuck spoonicorn.

I don't know how to help. There's no magic I can cast that will protect us from this dragon.

So I do what I've seen Moxie do a hundred times. I throw myself in front of my friends. Not like that's going to help anyone. I'll just get barbecued half a second before they do.

But hey. It's the thought that counts.

"Hurry, guys!" The dragon is almost upon us. The wind from his wings sends my hat sailing. He inhales, ready to unleash fire and rage down from above.

At that moment, the morning sun peeks over the mountain. The light is blinding.

And with my eyes squeezed tight, I suddenly know what to do.

I rip open my robes.

RHINESTONE ROCK STAR!

The morning light makes me shine like a thousand suns. Glacierbane screams and turns away from the glory of my bling.

Moxie slams her hammer against the cobbles, freeing the spoonicorn's hoof. "Got it!" she cries.

We dive through the front gate. The dragon lobs a ball of fire breath into the hole after us, but it's half-hearted. He knows from experience that he can't fit in that hole.

"MISERABLE MAGGOTS!" he roars. "WHERE DO YOU THINK YOU CAN GO THAT I WILL NOT FIND YOU?" There's a mighty whoosh of air. He's flying around. Back to his hole in the roof. He's going to smoke us out from the inside.

"You guys!" Sparkles cries. "You came back for me. You, like, literally came back for me!"

"Be quiet!" cries Moxie, running hard. "We're not talking to you!" But spoonicorns aren't known for their listening skills.

"Fart!" Sparkles says. "You totally saved me with your fashion sense." She nuzzles me affectionately. "You're wearing the outfit I got you! I can't even believe it!"

I push her away. "Get off me," I say. "I'm dressing in layers, that's all. It's cold up here."

Following Moxie through the wrecked entrance hall, we charge past the crumbling walls and scorched banners, back into the abandoned city. The canal runs through the center, its banks overflowing with a river of gold coins and sparkling gems.

"We need to hide," says Pan.

"And quick!" I say. I estimate we've got about two

minutes before the dragon comes barreling through the roof, all doom and gloom, toenails and bad breath.

Snomish buildings and workshops, homes and stores loom around us. A tower of glass rises from the center of the city, supporting the shattered roof far above. A million places to hide. But nowhere to be safe.

"We need someplace where he won't think to look for us," says Pan. "Something he won't burn to the ground. Until we can figure out what to do."

"Hurry!" I say, watching the sky nervously.

"I've got it," says Moxie with a grin.

CANNONBALL!

CHAPTER TWENTY-SIX

I've made a couch fort before.

A blanket fort.

Heck, one time I made a
fort out of lawn chairs and a
bunch of Master Elmore's
nightshirts. He was not
pleased.

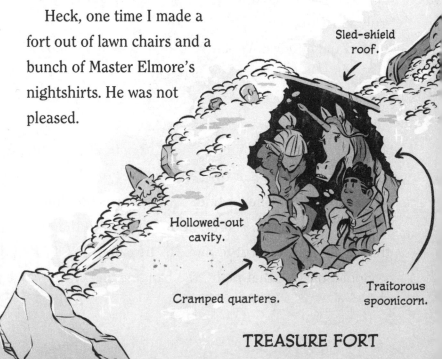

Sled-shield
roof.

Hollowed-out
cavity.

Cramped quarters.

Traitorous
spoonicorn.

TREASURE FORT

But I've never had a solid-gold treasure fort. Ooh là là. *Très* fancy.

"You guys," whispers Sparkles. "I—"

"Be quiet," says Moxie tensely.

"I'm so sorry," the spoonicorn tries again. "I—"

"You're not sorry you lied to us," I hiss. "You're sorry you got caught."

"No, seriously, guys," she says. "I—"

Pan clamps the spoonicorn's snout shut, fire burning in her elven eyes. "Sparkles, either zip your lip or I will hand-feed you to Glacierbane myself."

This shuts her up. And probably scars her for life. Pan doesn't get mad often, but when she does . . . it's truly terrifying.

We hunker down. We burrow in. And we don't move.

For twenty-four hours.

The first twelve hours are filled with crashes. Flames. Angry curses as Glacierbane searches the city for us. We lie still. Silent. Trying not to make a peep from our little nook. It's the worst game of hide-and-seek ever.

But the dragon never finds us. He burns buildings. He scorches bridges. But he never sets fire to the one thing that matters most to him. His treasure.

Sometime late that night, the banging and crashing

stops. Fire and fury turn to silence. But in my mind I picture Glacierbane hovering silently over Tinkertop. Watching. Waiting for us to reveal ourselves so he can swoop down and devour us.

So we don't move.

"I hope that TickTock is all right." They're the first whispered words that have been spoken in hours. And it's Sparkles who says them.

Sparkles the liar. Sparkles the traitor. Sparkles the jerk. And worst of all right now, Sparkles the fort hog.

"What do you care?" I hiss.

"I like that little phibling," she says meekly. "Come on, guys. Please. If it weren't for me, we would have starved to death by now."

I don't know about all that. But after a full day of being buried in treasure eating nothing but rainbow sherbet pops, starvation is starting to sound pretty good.

"Fart," says Moxie softly. "I'm sorry we doubted you."

"Yes," says Pan. "Your instincts were right not to trust Sparkles and Seraphim."

Sparkles shifts uncomfortably in the treasure pile. "I'm sitting right here, you know."

But Pan ignores her. "We said you were just jealous of them. But we were wrong."

Her words linger in the air.

"No, you weren't," I finally whisper back. "I *was* jealous of them." There's no denying it. I felt left out. Forgotten. Replaced. "I missed it being just us."

Moxie reaches through the gold and grabs my hand. "We're going to meet other people along the way," she says.

I feel Pan reach for my other hand. "But that will never change our friendship with you," she whispers.

I hesitate, trying to find the right words. "But it kind of did," I say nervously. "Pan, you sparred with Seraphim. And, Moxie, you window-shopped with her. It's bad enough she was better than me at everything. But those are *our* things."

I rub my eyes with my sleeve. "I know you're allowed to do stuff with other people. But you did *our* stuff . . . and you left *me* out."

There's a long still silence. "You're right, Fart," whispers Moxie. "Gosh, I'm so sorry."

"Me too," says Pan, squeezing my hand.

"Aw," says Sparkles. "Come on, you guys. Group hug!"

"Shush, horsey," says Moxie. "We may have saved your life. But we're still not talking to you." But I hear the slight grin in her voice. Only a real friend would notice it. And I do. And I find myself grinning too.

SUPERHEROIC ACHIEVEMENT!
Deep Talks with Friends!
(350 Experience Points Awarded)

Somebody moves slightly, and our shield-roof shifts, letting a little light into our dark burrow. The city is still.

"What do you say we try to get out of here?" I suggest.

"We need a plan," says Pan. "But you are right. We cannot stay here forever."

"That's for sure," says Moxie. "I gotta stretch. My muscles are cramped up."

Reaching out, she slides the shield aside ever so softly. Our eyes dart above us, searching for a flash of red scales, a spark of flame, anything that will tell us that we've been spotted.

But all is quiet. The skies are dragon-free.

And then Sparkles sniffs the air. "Wait!" she hisses. "Do you smell that?"

"What?" I whisper in panic. "Is it the dragon?"

"No," the spoonicorn says. "It's something else. Something ... dis-GUST-ing."

"I smell it too," says Pan, pulling herself cautiously from the coins. "That, my friends, is the smell of poop. Dragon poop."

Sparkles wrinkles her nose. "Oh my gosh. It is. It totally is."

Pan smiles. "And it's still fresh."

CHAPTER TWENTY-SEVEN

Fresh dragon doody.

Turds.

Poop.

Caca.

Dookie.

I never thought I'd be so happy to see a big pile of poo. But I am. I really am.

Pan pulls herself out of our fort and sneaks across the river of gold without making a peep.

The rest of us are not as noiseless. We unearth ourselves, coins clinking and treasure plinking alarmingly loud. But still there's no sign of Glacierbane.

"Maybe he's not home," Moxie whispers hopefully.

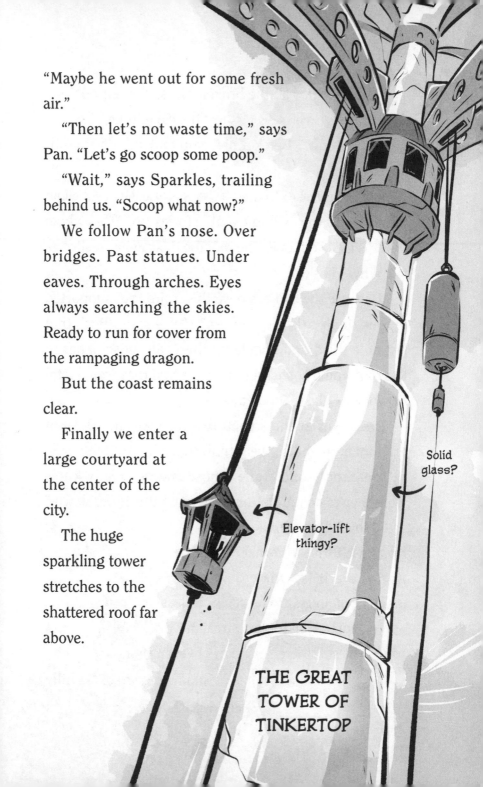

"Maybe he went out for some fresh air."

"Then let's not waste time," says Pan. "Let's go scoop some poop."

"Wait," says Sparkles, trailing behind us. "Scoop what now?"

We follow Pan's nose. Over bridges. Past statues. Under eaves. Through arches. Eyes always searching the skies. Ready to run for cover from the rampaging dragon.

But the coast remains clear.

Finally we enter a large courtyard at the center of the city.

The huge sparkling tower stretches to the shattered roof far above.

Solid glass?

Elevator-lift thingy?

THE GREAT TOWER OF TINKERTOP

"Watch out for all the broken glass," I point out.

"It's not glass," says Moxie. "It's clearstone."

"Clearstone?" I pick a piece up and rub its smooth surface.

"Arkanium. Like Pan's staff," says Moxie. Her eyes climb the tower to the ceiling twenty stories up. "This whole tower is made out of it. The roof too. It's genius, really."

"Why?" I ask.

"Because the snomes have the entire roof supported by this single arkanium tower," Moxie says. "With that big hole the dragon made up there, all those panes in the roof would come crumbling down if they were metal or wood or glass. Too heavy."

She stares at the structure with respect. "But not arkanium. Incredibly beautiful, super lightweight, crystal clear, but solid stone. These snomes really know what they're doing. Nothing will bring this tower down."

Following the curve of the tower, we turn the corner. And there it is. Our moment of poop is at hand.

"Ew," says Sparkles. "That's narsty."

But somebody has beaten us to it.

Anton.

He chitters loudly at us, defending his find with waving feelers and a karate-chop attitude.

"Tell that overgrown bug to be quiet!" hisses Moxie, scanning the skies.

I cast my Magic Mouth spell and rush forward, clamping my hand over Anton's chittering mouthhole. "Be quiet!" I whisper in his clicky language. "It's just us!"

"This is mine!" he whispers. "I know it looks delicious! I know there's probably enough for everyone to have a bite! But back off! Because I haven't had boom-boom this fresh in years!"

"We don't want your boom-boom," I tell him.

"Oh. Well, good." And he turns back to his meal.

"We want what's in it," I tell him.

"What's in it?" He stops, confused. "There's nothing in it but solid nutrition. And a rich, tangy flavor. And that oh-so-decadent mouthfeel that reminds you of the Sunday poo dinners Mama used to make."

I gag slightly. "Yes, there is," I say. "And we need your help to get it."

Anton is happy as a pig in mud. As a hog in slop. As a filth feaster in dragon droppings.

After promising him he could keep all the poo to himself, Anton happily burrows through the pile for us, searching for anything of value.

The spoonicorn can't take it. She gags and tiptoes around the corner to "keep watch." For the rest of us, it's hard to keep our eyes open, but we're all eagerly hoping that somewhere, somehow, there's a digested magic item in this heap.

SERAPHIM'S ARMOR

After a few initial dives into the pile, the filth feaster throws something muck-covered and metal to the ground. Something that sends a nasty shock through us all. Something that reminds us exactly what this meal consisted of.

I don't know why it never occurred to me. There's a reason Glacierbane hasn't made a doo-doo for years. Until today.

Because yesterday, for the first time in ages, the dragon ate something. Or rather, someone.

"Well," says Moxie, gulping back a gag. "That's unfortunate."

"There's more!" says Anton. He unearths something long and thin.

Seraphim's bow.

From here a number of random undigestibles come flying out. A belt buckle. Arrowheads. Earrings. None of it magical. None of it any use to us.

Anton emerges. "One last thing." Something long and thin dangles from one of his many legs. Through the filth it's hard to know what it is. But then Pan lets out a gasp of recognition.

"My mother's necklace," she whispers.

The journey through the dragon's digestive super-highway has changed the necklace. Magnified its magic. Intensified its enchantment. Because according to my ring of magic detection, this is now one mondo magic item.

"That's it," I tell them. "A poop-powered magic item."

"The only one in the pile." Moxie looks at Pan nervously. "I guess it's a good thing that Seraphim stole your necklace."

"I guess so," Pan says. She reaches out and takes the necklace from Anton, wiping it clean on a rag.

Suddenly Sparkles comes galloping up. "We've got company!" she hisses.

We dive into the shadows and stare skyward. There floating noiselessly on the breeze far above us . . .

Glacierbane.

"YOU CANNOT HIDE FOREVER!" he roars in frustration. "I KNOW YOU ARE HERE, YOU COWARDLY VILLAINS! AND SOONER OR LATER YOU WILL HAVE TO COME OUT AND FACE ME! THERE IS NO ESCAPE TO BE HAD!"

"Oh dang," cries Anton. "Later, guys!" He burrows into his poo pile and disappears from sight.

"The dragon is right," says Pan solemnly. "Even if we could escape unseen, we have no way off the island. We are trapped."

I hug the tower tightly, fingernails scraping against the smooth glasslike surface.

Glasslike. But not glass.

Clearstone. Clear . . . stone.

My wheels start turning fast. "Moxie, did you say this whole tower and the entire roof is made from solid clearstone?"

"Yep," she says. "Rock solid. Not even dragon fire could bring that bad boy down."

A big smile washes over my face. "Moxie. You should know by now. Things are not always as they seem."

I circle the tower, approaching the elevator-lift thingy. "Do you think you can get this thing working?" I ask Moxie, pointing to the pulleys and levers. "Get us up to the top?"

Moxie examines the lift. "Yeah, I think so."

I climb in. "Then come on."

"Where are we going?" asks Pan, scrambling in behind me.

I just grin at my friends. "Do you trust me?"

"No question," says Pan.

"You bet," says Moxie.

"Like eighty-four percent," says Sparkles.

Stupid spoonicorn.

"Well then," I say. "Get ready to slay a dragon."

CHAPTER TWENTY-EIGHT

The domed roof of Tinkertop is much higher than it looks.

Moxie's not TickTock. And she's definitely no snome. But she seems to under-stand enough of their ticktock-y, knock-knocky gizmos to get the lift working. "It's just a counterweight system," she says.

I don't know what that means. All I know is that the ride up the tower is smooth and quiet. We make it to the top without the dragon spotting us. And that's all that counts.

From up here we can see everything. Glacierbane floats noiselessly below us, circling the city, eyes searching. It never occurs to him to look up.

"Tell us what to do," Pan says simply. She looks at me unquestioningly. I'm not gonna lie, it's a nice feeling.

"Well . . ." I hesitate, not sure how to say it. "I have a plan. But it requires . . . bait."

"Bait?" asks Moxie.

"Bait?" asks Pan.

"Bait?" asks Sparkles.

"Bait," I confirm. "To lure the dragon. And it can't be me."

Moxie and Pan glance at each other. I can see it. They're both about to step up, each one ready to lay it on the line for the rest of us.

"I'll do it," she says.

But it's not Moxie. And it's not Pan.

It's **Sp✰rkles**. With a ✰ instead of an *a*.

She hangs her head. "Truthfully," she says softly, "I would have left you, just like Seraphim. And still you guys came back for me."

She lifts her head and meets my gaze. "Nobody's ever come back for me. The least I can do is be bait."

I'm speechless. This doesn't sound like the spoonicorn I've come to know and despise.

She shrugs and tosses her mane. "Besides. I'm the only one that doesn't smell like dookie. No offense."

And . . . there she is.

"Fair enough," I tell her. "Get on the lift and we'll lower you down."

"Like a worm on a hook," says Pan.

"Exactly," I say.

"Ew. Don't say 'worm,'" says Sparkles, climbing back into the elevator. "Lower me down like a shining disco ball on a string."

"Sure. Whatever," I tell her. "When I give you the signal, start making a ruckus. Get the dragon to come for you."

"Got it," she says. "I'll turn on all the charm. And then you'll yank me out of there. Right?"

I glance at Moxie, and she nods.

"Sure," I say. "In theory."

"In theory?"

I shrug. "What can I tell you? You'll just have to trust me."

She admires my glittering rhinestone jumpsuit. "In that outfit, I do. I really do."

I nod to Moxie, and she throws the mechanism. Sparkles descends slowly down the side of the tower. Once she's about halfway, we bring the lift to a halt.

Moxie assures me she can make it come back up quickly when the time is right. By cutting the rope connected to the counterweight system. Or something.

"Get ready," I tell Pan and Moxie. "Make sure you're not standing on anything made of clearstone. Only metal."

"What exactly is about to happen?" asks Pan.

I hold up a roll of parchment. My last remaining magic scroll. "Things are about to get seriously cheesy."

I take a deep breath. I catch the spoonicorn's eye. I nod.

And then we hear it. Echoing through the empty city. The spoonicorn . . . is singing.

"If you wanna be my baaaaaaaay-beeeeeee!
Yeah! Yeah!
All you gotta do,
Is shake your scaly booooooot-eeeee that
waaaaay!

Yeah! Yeah! Yeeeeee-aaaaaaah, boy!"

Oh my gosh. It's some kind of weird mermaid hip-hop. And it's hideous.

"Hey!" says Moxie. "She's not half-bad."

I like this dwarf. But we clearly have very different opinions about music.

Sparkles has caught the dragon's attention. He jerks his great horned head, eyes seeking out the source of the sound.

"And, girl! Don'tchoo
Be jealous of my bo-daaaaaaay!
No! No!
And girl! Don'tchoo
Be jealous of the way I make my tail swaaaay!
No! No! Noooo, girl!"

You gotta give her credit. She's really going for it.

The dragon spots her. Terror runs through me as he spreads his wings, swallowing the city behind him.

"NEFARIOUS WRETCH!" he bellows, hurling himself toward the spoonicorn. "NOW I HAVE YOU!"

"Get ready, Moxie," I say, spreading open the scroll in my hands.

The dragon flies at the tower. "YOU WERE MISTAKEN TO REVEAL YOURSELF TO ME! AND NOW YOU SHALL BURN!" He sucks inward, preparing to unleash his fiery fury upon the helpless spoonicorn.

"Now!" I cry.

Moxie slices the rope, freeing the counterweight. The lift flies skyward.

Glacierbane's eyes dart upward, following the rocketing spoonicorn. To the domed clearstone ceiling. To us.

I lock eyes with
the malevolent beast.
A smile seeps across
his serpent face at the
sight of us. The rest of
his prey. His mighty
wings flap, sending
him soaring skyward. Straight at us.

I am frozen in fear. Mesmerized by this beast from my
darkest nightmares.

"Now, Fart!" cries Pan.

"Whatever you're going to do!" roars Moxie, snatching the spoonicorn from the lift. "Do it now!"

The voices of my friends melt through my terror. The
great dragon inhales, preparing to flood fire across the
roof, the tower, and us.

I look at the scroll. I touch the clearstone roof. And I say the incantation:

"Obsidiana mozzarella
Scoria langoria
Gouda'sinsalt graphitite e solbasalt
Mascarpone sau-rennet, solido por curdsinwhey!"

Magically the ceiling, the tower—everything made of clearstone—transforms. Stone replaced . . . by cheese.

Ooey-gooey, oh-so-chewy string cheese.

The dragon launches his blazing breath skyward. But the flames never reach us.

Instantly heated by the fiery flames, the cheese melts immediately into a thick liquidy mass.

A sheet of scalding-hot goo drops down, dousing the shooting flames. It hits the dragon, blanketing his face, coating his claws, gumming up his wings.

The melting tower topples, enveloping the dragon in gooey goodness.

Queso con draco. And me with no chips to dip.

CHAPTER TWENTY-NINE

The entire city shakes with the force of Glacierbane's fall.

And our world starts to crumble.

I immediately see the flaw in my plan. The fly in the ooey-gooey ointment. My own lack of gnomish know-how.

The metal girders that crisscross the roof—the ones we're standing on—are supported at the edges of the city by bronze towers. That's good.

But the central support tower is gone. A gooey pool down below us. So there's nothing to hold it all up. The metal girders shake and sway precariously.

In other words . . . it's only a matter of seconds before we're going down.

"It was a good plan, Fart!" roars Moxie, holding on to Sparkles. Even now, with the girders starting to give way under her, Moxie is grinning.

"The best!" says Pan with a grim smile.

"I give it a five out of ten!" cries Sparkles. "Would not recommend!"

I can't help but laugh. Stupid spoonicorn.

I look to the sky. After the long hours we spent in our dark hidey-hole, I want one more glimpse of sunlight before I drop to my doom.

But something blots out the sun. I shield my eyes as a huge shape fills the sky, shrouding us in terrible shadow.

Another dragon! Unfair! Nobody ever said anything about a Glacierbane Jr.!

But it's not a dragon. It's . . .

A cluster of balloons?

No. Not balloons.

Float-fish.

A whole flock. And dangling below them, held aloft by dozens of ropes . . . a ship. A floating ship.

No. A *squilsevlar*.

An airship.

And there at the helm . . . is Knock-Knock.

The structure below us begins to collapse. Metal beams rain down on the snomish city. And we're next.

Something smacks me in the face. A rope.

"Friends! Be grabbing on! Fast-quick!"

I know that froggy little voice. It's TickTock! He's tossed us a lifeline.

Pan grabs on effortlessly. But the rope bobbles out of my reach. There's no time to dillydally. As the last girder gives out from under me, I leap. Flying through the air, I latch on to the rope a few feet below Pan.

Below me, Moxie manages to grab the rope. She grips it one-handed, struggling to hold on.

Because her other hand is full. Of spoonicorn.

Having hooves instead of hands is a major disadvantage right now. Sparkles is bundled into Moxie's free arm like a sack of super-obnoxious groceries.

And Moxie . . . is slipping.

"Moxie!" I cry. "Hold on!"

"Moxie!" Pan shouts. "Don't you dare let go!"

I want to scream out to her. To tell her to drop that spoonicorn. To save herself. But I can't make myself say the words. All I can do is watch.

"Told you I was a good singer," Sparkles tells Moxie. "Did you see that dragon come running for an autograph? Total fanboy."

"Be quiet!" grunts Moxie, gritting her teeth with effort.

TickTock is hauling us up. We're rising. But slowly.

Not quick enough for Moxie.

"Moxie," says Sparkles softly. "Let me go, sis."

"No!" roars Moxie.

But the spoonicorn smiles. "It's okay. I've dragged you down long enough."

Sparkles sighs. "Thanks for trying. It's more than I deserve."

And with that she wriggles herself free of Moxie's arms. And starts to fall.

Lightning-quick, Moxie loops her foot around the rope. She lets go and dives, reaching . . . stretching . . . grabbing.

YOINK!

There they dangle. Like a disco ball on a string.

CHAPTER THIRTY

From the safety of the *squilsevlar*, we stare down at the mess we've made.

Tinkertop's beautiful domed roof is gone. Buildings are scorched with dragon fire. And the streets are filled with cheese.

But Glacierbane is dead.

SUPERHEROIC ACHIEVEMENT!
Slay a Dragon!
(3,000 Experience
Points Awarded)

The snomes will be able to return home. Sure, they'll have a few DIY projects to do. But they have the know-how to fix it up better than ever. And the cash. After all, the river runs with gold.

And the streets run with string cheese. I hope they aren't lactose intolerant.

"I just have one thing to say," mutters Sparkles.

"How about 'thank you'?" I suggest.

"How about 'I'm sorry'?" says Pan, eyebrows arched.

"How about 'I owe you one'?" adds Moxie with a grin.

"Yes," says the spoonicorn. "All those. But also one other thing."

She turns to look at her refection in the shiny metal hull.

"Oh. My. Gosh. You totally bent my spoon! Like, literally."

With Bizzy leading the way and the float-fish following along hungrily, Knock-Knock turns the ship toward Meanwhile. As we leave Tinkertop behind, Tick-Tock and Knock-Knock regale us with the story of their adventure.

They found Grease-Ratchet's battle-bot in the Great Workshop.

Turns out the Great Workshop held more than battle-bots.

Like airships.

The mechanical doohickeys that keep these tubs afloat has long since rusted away.

But Bizzy makes great float-fish bait.

They managed to lasso enough to get the ship floating. And to give us a way off the air island.

This fish-powered *squilsevlar* isn't fast. But it sure beats trudging through the snow.

When we arrive at Meanwhile, the snomes welcome us like returning heroes.

They ooh at the sight of our fish-fueled vessel. They aah at the return of Grease-Ratchet's battle-bot.

But they are rendered speechless when we tell them that Glacierbane is dead. That Tinkertop is theirs once again.

Then they cry.

Then they cheer.

Then they feast. I stuff myself with cave-grown mushrooms. I gorge myself on rack of winter wolf.

I pass on the yeti-on-a-stick. Too many bad memories.

And I definitely avoid the cheese plate.

When we tell the snomes the story about luring the dragon to its doom, they demand to hear the song Sparkles sang.

Turns out snomes really have a thing for weird mermaid hip-hop. They go gaga for her voice. She is a triple threat after all.

1. Annoying.
2. Obnoxious.
3. And a decent singer.

It's probably good that they can't understand the lyrics.

The snomes look upon Knock-Knock with new respect. They suddenly realize that there's more to Knock-Knock than some language skills and really big glasses. She is clever. And heroic. And one heck of a bee pilot. Plus she has helped free their beloved Tinkertop from the clutches of an evil dragon. And provided them with a lifetime supply of mozzarella. In a grand ceremony, Knock-Knock is crowned vice-boss-king.

GVIGVILI!!!

After a week of festivities and feasting, resting and recuperating, we prepare our airship for departure. Ever since our adventures on the high seas, Pan has wanted a ship. Looks like we have one now. It's not the ship she imagined. It's ten times better.

As we load up for the voyage home, Sparkles and the snomes come out to greet us.

"So what's your plan?" Moxie asks the spoonicorn. "Are you coming with us?"

The spoonicorn's mouth hangs open. "You'd let me come with you?" she asks in shock. "After I tried to betray you?"

"It's true. You are a traitorous wretch," says Moxie with a slight grin. "No offense."

"But you also tried to save us," says Pan solemnly. "We'd be happy to have you come with us. That is, if Fart agrees." Pan puts her arm around me. "After all, the three of us do things together. Or not at all."

It brings a tear to the eye. It really does.

"Well? Banana Boy?" asks the spoonicorn, eyeing me cautiously.

I sigh. This shiny pony has been a pain in my patootie from day one. Now's my shot. To give her what she really deserves.

A second chance. I guess everyone deserves one. Even stupid spoonicorns.

"Calm your hooves," I tell her. "You can come if you really want to."

"Wow," says Sparkles. "Just wow. Thanks, guys." She looks around at the snomes that have gathered to say goodbye. "But I think I'll stick around here for a while. Maybe help my fans relocate to Tinkertop. I don't think they could handle it if I left."

When Knock-Knock translates that the spoonicorn is staying, the snomes all cheer. Then they break out into the ever-popular mermaid hip-hop classic "Shake That Scaly Booty." Complete with dance moves.

"Snomes! Am I right? I literally love these guys!" Sparkles says with a snort. As far as they're concerned, she's just a weird horse with a bent spoon, a good voice, and an endless supply of sherbet pops.

"Don't they realize how beautiful you are?" Moxie asks with a grin.

Sparkles smiles softly. "They don't seem to care."

CHAPTER THIRTY-ONE

We wave farewell to the snomes. TickTock gives Knock-Knock a heartfelt hug goodbye. The sun is shining as we take to the skies, Bizzy leading the way.

After all, we owe Kevin a certain poop-scented necklace. And Pan has a family reunion to get to.

The Fourteen Realms unfurl like a map below us.

"Fart," says Pan softly. "I told Seraphim the story about my mom. But I didn't tell you."

"I know," I admit. "I heard."

She bites her lip uncertainly. "I was worried you'd get upset about the whoopee-cushion-fart part. About how that's what got my mother killed. I know how you love farts."

I think about this for a minute. It did feel crummy to get left out like that. But then I realize something. "It's your story to share," I tell her. "Or not. We are best friends. But that doesn't mean you owe it to me to share that story."

She smiles gently. "That is exactly why you are the right person to share it with. I won't forget that."

TickTock steers the ship. The three of us stand quietly at the rail, taking in the view.

"It's been over three weeks since we left Kevin's tower," I realize.

"Gosh!" says Moxie. "Has it really? So much has happened!"

"We survived the Arch Angel," says Pan.

"Slayed a dragon," Moxie adds.

"Crossed the Frostflung Mountains and lived to tell the tale," I chime in.

"Rooted around in dragon dookie and emerged victorious," says Moxie with a grin.

She's right. So much has happened. It's only been a month. But we are not the same Level 3 heroes that set out from Kevin's tower. I feel something inside me shift.

**CONGRATULATIONS!
LEVEL UP!**
You are now Level 4!

I sense a new level of power and knowledge swell within me. I can somehow tell that my best magic is just ahead. But something ominous clouds my mind as well. Because with great power . . . come great dangers.

The next day, Conklin comes into view. And beyond that, we see it . . . peeking out among the trees in the distance. Kevin's tower.

Pan fingers her necklace thoughtfully. It's been washed and thoroughly sterilized. It's back on her neck where it belongs.

"What do you think Kevin is going to do with the necklace now that it's all dragon-dookie-supercharged?" I ask my friends. "Do you really think he needs it to make an ointment for his mom?"

Moxie bites her lip thoughtfully. "We heard them talking about burning some plants, right?"

"Tolivar and verbena," says Pan softly.

"Yeah, that's right," says Moxie. "Maybe his backyard is overrun. Maybe he's making a weed killer." She turns to Pan. "What do you think, Pan?"

The elf sighs softly. "Honestly I don't think I care what he does with it. As long as he keeps his promise."

She's thinking about her mom. I know that. Heck, I know these guys better than anybody. And they know me. And I realize that nothing . . . and nobody . . . can ever change that.

"My father always said this necklace would draw me close to my mother," Pan says softly, gazing down at the approaching tower. "But now that its power has been intensified by the dragon, I really feel it."

"Feel what?" I ask.

She strokes the necklace, lost in thought. "That it's been drawing me there all this time," she finally says, pointing to Kevin's tower. "Right from the beginning."

She turns to us, pointed eyebrows raised. "Do you think the necklace has been leading me to my mother? That it somehow knew Kevin could bring her back to me?"

Moxie, TickTock, and I just shake our heads. We have no answers.

None of us know what mysterious secrets await us in the tower. What adventures lie just ahead. But whatever it is, the four of us will face it side by side.

I breathe a sigh of relief as the tower looms into view. We're almost home.

And then it hits me: no, not home.

Me, Moxie, Pan, and TickTock are together.

Whatever faces us next . . . we're already home.

Headmaster Verbina should NEVER have let me graduate. I wasn't ready.

And now, because of me, Cypress Silversnow is dead.

I'm somewhere in the woods of Blackrook Reach. Hiding. But in the distance, I can hear a hideous wail. Maybe it's the manticore, looking for me. Or maybe it's something even worse.

I think Cypress had a husband. And a little daughter.

If I ever get out of this mess, I'm gonna go to the elven kingdom of Kirajoy. I'll look her husband in the face. And tell him what I did. I owe Cypress that much.

I've been such an idiot. Such a dork. Such a fool. But not anymore.

From now on, I'm gonna be serious about my magic. About everything.

I'm not Tolivar Elmore anymore. As far as I'm concerned, he's dead. Like Cypress.

From here on out, I'm gonna do everything I can to be Elmore the . . . Worthy.

No. More than worthy. Elmore the . . . Admired.

No. Something that would make Cypress proud. Something that would even impress her.

Yeah. That's it.

Elmore . . . the Impressive.

(From the mage journal of Tolivar Elmore, age 12)

BEHIND THE SCENES WITH CAM KENDELL

An Illustration from Start to Finish

STEP 1:

It starts with a rough sketch to figure out where all the elements and characters go in the scene.

STEP 2:

In this step I clean up the sketch to figure out more of the details and character anatomy.

STEP 3:

Now I draw the final lines, making any changes Aaron or the editing team asks for.

STEP 4:

The last step is where the shading is added. And just like magic that takes a lot of time and work, the art appears!

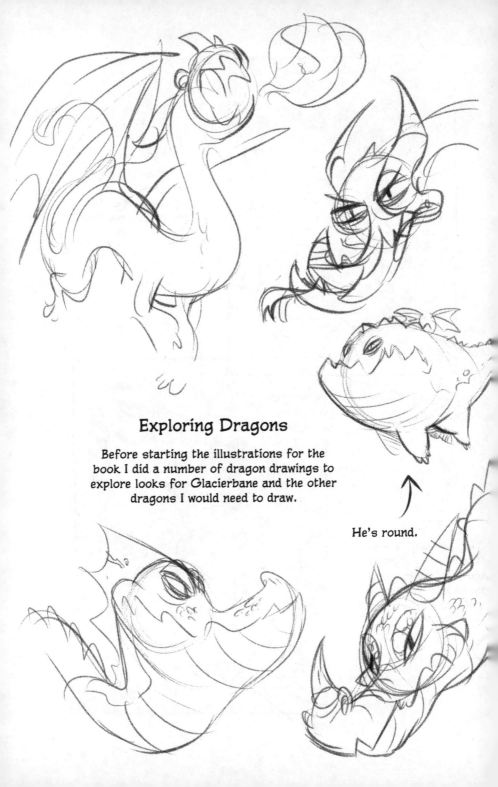

Exploring Dragons

Before starting the illustrations for the book I did a number of dragon drawings to explore looks for Glacierbane and the other dragons I would need to draw.

He's round.

The final Glacierbane design.

I gave Glacierbane an almost alligator-like build and a strong jaw so he would have an imposing presence.

Want to wield a bo staff like Pan,
swing a hammer like Moxie, or turn someone
into a stinky gas like Fart?

Check out
FART QUEST: THE GAME
to continue the smelly saga with our heroes!

Download it for free at
https://read.macmillan.com/mcpg/fart-quest/

And don't forget! There is
more Fart in your future!

**FART QUEST:
THE TROLL'S TOE CHEESE**

Available September 2022

AARON REYNOLDS is a #1 *New York Times*–bestselling author of many highly acclaimed books for kids, including the Caldecott Honor book *Creepy Carrots!*, *Nerdy Birdy*, *Dude!*, and *The Incredibly Dead Pets of Rex Dexter*. As a longtime Dungeon Master and lover of Dungeons & Dragons, Aaron is no stranger to epic quests. He lives in the Chicago area with his wife, two kids, four cats, and between zero and ten goldfish, depending on the day. **aaron-reynolds.com**

CAM KENDELL is an illustrator of all things absurd and fantastical; creator of comics such as *Choose Your Gnome Adventure*, *Mortimer B. Radley: The Case of the Missing Monkey Skull*, and *Flopnar the Bunbarian*; and artist for board games like D&D's Dungeon Mayhem: Monster Madness and 5-Minute Mystery. When not drawing gnomes and/or goblins, Cam enjoys birding, rocking on the accordion, losing at board games, and hiking in the beautiful Utah mountains with his wife and four children, hoping to see a black bear ... from a safe distance. **camkendell.com**